Books by Tristan Bancks

The Tom Weekly series

My Life and Other Stuff I Made Up

My Life and Other Stuff that Went Wrong

My Life and Other Massive Mistakes

My Life and Other Exploding Chickens

My Life and Other Weaponised Muffins

My Life and Other Failed Experiments
(yes, Tom Weekly is back with more weird, funny, gross,
BRAND-NEW adventures in July 2018!)

Two Wolves

The Fall

The Mac Slater series

Mac Slater, Coolhunter

Mac Slater, Imaginator

TOM WEEKLY

MY LIFE AND OTHER EXPLODING CHICKENS

AS TOLD TO
TRISTAN BANCKS
AND
GUS GORDON

RANDOM HOUSE AUSTRALIA

A Random House book
Published by Penguin Random House Australia Pty Ltd
Level 3, 100 Pacific Highway, North Sydney NSW 2060
www.penguin.com.au

Penguin
Random House
Australia

First published by Random House Australia in 2016
This edition published in 2018

Text copyright © Tristan Bancks 2016
Illustration copyright © Gus Gordon 2016

The moral right of the author and illustrator has been asserted.

Addresses for the Penguin Random House group of companies can be found
at global.penguinrandomhouse.com.

A catalogue record for this
book is available from the
NATIONAL
LIBRARY
OF AUSTRALIA
National Library of Australia

ISBN: 978 0 14379 011 2

Cover and internal illustrations by Gus Gordon
Cover design by Astred Hicks, designcherry
Internal design by Benjamin Fairclough © Penguin Random House Australia,
based on original series design by Astred Hicks, designcherry
Printed in Australia by Griffin Press, an accredited ISO AS/NZS 14001:2004
Environmental Management System printer

Random House Australia uses papers that are natural, renewable and
recyclable products and made from wood grown in sustainable forests.
The logging and manufacturing processes are expected to conform to the
environmental regulations of the country of origin.

Contents

Hey.

I'm Tom Weekly, and this is my fourth book of weird, funny, sometimes gross stories. Within these pages you will discover the answers to life's biggest questions. Stuff like:

1. How do I return a book that's five years overdue to the library without being attacked by Ninja Librarians?

2. How awesome will it be when I'm in a nursing home and wearing those cool, old-guy nappies?

3. Where do all the missing, odd socks go?

4. How do I stop that freaky person in my class from trying to kiss me?

5. And what should I do if an evil clown is trying to kill me?

I always look on the bright side of life.
When I come up with a genius idea, failure
is not an option.

But sometimes my dreams and hopes hit
the hen house of reality at 197 km/hour
and erupt like an exploding chicken.

Let my life be a warning to you.

Tom

STELLA HOLLING AND THE GREAT HOMEWORK SCAM

Homework is destroying my life. I think it should be banned. We do 30 hours of school each week, and then they want us to do more work at home? I don't think so. The worst part is that Mum hassles me about it all week, so I pretend I left my assignment at school, or I tell her about new research that claims homework causes blindness, and then I don't do it and I get detention.

Right now, though, at this very moment,

I have the opportunity to never do homework again. Ever.

I'm standing under the fig tree near the front gate. Hundreds of kids stream past, heading for their buses. I am spying on Stella Holling, who is tucked into a narrow gap between the Year Four and Five portables. Almost every kid in my class walks by and hands their homework to her. They make it look so easy. They give it to her, say, 'Thanks, Stella,' then walk away. Stella will do their homework for them – in their own handwriting – and get them full marks, no matter the subject. No questions asked.

Stella says she *loves* homework, and she's been offering this free service to her classmates for the past five weeks. (NB: For something big, like a model of the solar system or a family tree, she expects modest payment in the form of pink jelly beans or strawberry jelly crystals.)

I have not yet taken advantage of her offer because I smell a rat. Stella Holling has been in love with me since second grade. She has tricked, swindled and blackmailed me into kissing her so many times that I know there must be a catch. Stella is one of the most devious humans on the planet, especially when it comes to kissing me. There's no way that she would just do my homework out of the goodness of her heart.

Leilani, Jonah, Brittany – they all hand over their homework sheets and head off to their buses, happy as anything. They'll probably hang out with friends, kick balls, play video games and do bommies off Kings Bay wharf all afternoon, while I'm working my stinking guts out.

Stella is now cradling a large pile of papers, and she has an enormous smile on her face. She looks down at the pile like she wants to marry it. Maybe she really does just love homework.

The last few kids – Billy, Milo, Huxley and Jack – add their papers to Stella's stack. This cuts me deeply, knowing that Jack will

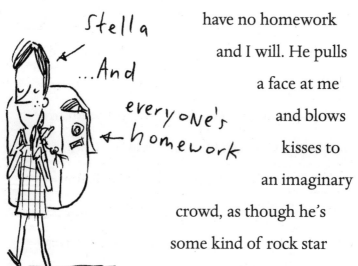

Stella

...And

everyone's

homework

have no homework and I will. He pulls a face at me and blows kisses to an imaginary crowd, as though he's some kind of rock star for having found a loophole in the education system. He bows to his invisible fans, then walks right over to me.

'You are one pathetic loser, Weekly.'

I growl.

'Would any girl really do almost their entire class's homework for *five weeks* just to kiss you? Most girls would do everyone's homework for five weeks *not* to have to kiss you. Think about it. Are you really that special?'

I think about it for a moment. And I really don't think I'm that special. It's just –

'I've gotta go,' Jack says. 'I might see if Lewis wants to go up to the oval.'

The thought of my two best friends free as birds while I sit at the kitchen table doing long division kills me. I don't have a choice. I have to take the plunge, risk everything. I start towards Stella, pulling my homework out of my bag.

'Yes!' Jack says, pumping his fist, following me. 'That's awesome. Do you want to play soccer or footy? Or do you want to come over to my house and –'

'Stella!' I say.

She looks up.

A NEW scientific study HAS revealed a disturbing link between HOMEWORK and the BUBONIC plague. Also MAD cow disease, irritable bowel syndrome, tinea and DEATh. PIckiNg your nose is still okay.

NEWS

I glance around, making sure that no teachers are watching.

I hold out my homework.

She looks at me for an uncomfortably long time. Then she smiles, just like she did with the others.

'Sure,' she says. She takes the paper from my hand.

'Thanks,' I say, then Jack and I turn and walk away.

And that's it. I can't believe how easy it was.

I walk slightly faster than usual, putting as much space between Stella and me as possible, just in case, but I can't help grinning so wide my jaw aches. Jack puts his hand out and I give him five. 'You should have done that *weeks* ago,' he says. 'Why don't you get off at my stop and –'

'Oh, To-om!' says a voice from behind us.

My smile wilts. I pretend not to hear. We continue towards the front gate, picking up speed.

'Tommyyy!' Stella says, louder this time.

Up ahead I can see Mrs Hamilton standing next to my bus, talking to the driver. She looks my way.

'TOM!' Stella calls and, this time, her voice cuts through everything. There's no way that I could not have heard her. She's only about 20 metres behind us. I don't want her getting weird, so I stop. I turn. I look at her. I am reminded of a spider that I once saw catching a fly in the window frame above my bed. I can feel the sticky web beneath my feet. She creeps out from between the classrooms. I wait for her to start wrapping me up before sinking her fangs in. Every organ in my body screams *RUN!*

'My bus is about to go,' I call out. 'I've gotta –'

'Uh-uh-uh!' she says, shaking her head and waggling her finger.

I start to worry that she might do something bad to my homework, like put lipstick kisses in the margin, or answer '1 + 1= Us', or dob me in. I move slowly back towards her. I stop a couple of metres away, just out of kissing range. The grin on her face is truly terrifying.

'I just have one incy-wincy little request,' she says.

'What?' I ask, but I already know.

'One ickle kissy for Stella?' she says, fluttering her eyelashes. 'In exchange for doing your homework.'

I take a long, slow breath, trying to swallow the nuclear explosion happening inside me.

'No one else has to kiss you,' I say through gritted teeth.

She shrugs. 'I don't *want* to kiss anyone else.'

'That's not fair,' I say.

'Fair schmair,' she says.

'I've told you a hundred times that my heart belongs to Sasha.'

Stella scrunches her fists at the mention of my true love. 'And I've told you a hundred *and one* times that your heart belongs to *me*.' She says this in a way that makes me feel she may actually have plans to remove my heart at some stage.

'That's it. Give me back my homework.'

'Nope.'

'Whaddya mean "nope"?' I reach to grab my sheet from the top of the pile, but she pulls it away.

The enforcer.

'What's goin' on?' says a booming voice from behind me. I look around and up. It's Brent Bunder, the biggest kid in our school, looming over me. Just what I need. He smells like a sickening mix of fish from Bunder's Fish Shop and body odour. Brent is taller than most of the teachers. He's had a moustache since before he was born. He also wants me dead, ever since Jack and I tricked him into giving us free hot chips from his parents' shop.

'Nothing,' I say.

Brent hands his homework to Stella and says, 'Thanks, Holling.'

'If you don't kiss me, Tom,' Stella says, 'I not only won't do *your* homework – I won't do *anyone's*.'

'What?' I look at Jack, then up at Brent, hoping for backup. 'That's ridiculous.'

'One kiss every Monday afternoon and everything will continue to run smoothly,' she says.

'No way! I'll just get *Sasha* to help me with my homework.'

The liquid in her eyeballs starts to boil. I'm sure I can hear a faint whistle coming from her ears. I've got her now.

'I'd hate to have to tell the rest of the class who ruined the sweet homework deal, Husband,' she says.

'I'm *not* your husband!'

'You will be one day.' She winks and turns my spine to ice. She hands Brent his homework. 'Sorry, Brent. You'll have to do it yourself.'

A very large hand grabs the back of my shirt. 'Kiss her,' Brent says.

'But –'

'Pucker *up*,' he says, close to my ear now, low and menacing.

Stella finds Jack's homework. 'There you go,' she says, handing it to him. 'I guess I'll give the others their blank sheets back tomorrow, after it's due. Oh, well, it was good while it lasted.'

Jack glares samurai swords at me.

Stella smiles.

Brent's grip on my shirt tightens, making breathing slightly difficult.

'Alright, I'll kiss her,' I wheeze.

Brent releases his grip.

I squeeze my eyes closed and try to magic myself back over behind the tree, before Jack wrecked my life by telling me that Stella meant no harm.

I open my eyes. I am staring at Stella Holling's smooshed-out lips. She's waiting.

Brent shoves me in the back and I move in towards her. I promised myself that I would never kiss her again and yet, somehow, here I am, centimetres from her face. I have goosebumps on my skin and it's the middle of summer. My heart does a drum roll. A pool of acid burns a hole in my stomach.

Stella's lips are all dry and flaky. And she has red stuff glistening at the corners of her mouth – red frog residue. She's been eating frogs from the canteen again. Stella goes cuckoo when she eats sugar, and red food colouring makes it nine times worse.

'Kissy, kissy!' she singsongs, making a smooching sound with her lips. Brent pokes me in the back with one of his gigantic fingers, and I am so close to Stella's face I can see myself reflected in her wild, glassy eyes.

All this, just to get out of doing long division. Now that I have to kiss Stella every Monday for the rest of my school life, homework doesn't seem that bad. What was I so worried about? It only takes me half an hour a week, but I might need years of therapy to get over kissing Stella 256 times between now and high school graduation.

Not to mention the lip transplant. I'd be happy to do everyone in the class's homework *not* to have to do this.

I run that line through my head one more time. *I'd be happy to do everyone in the class's homework* not *to have to do this.*

I really would.

With a millimetre to go before my lips touch the most radioactive substance known to humankind – Stella's saliva – I pull back and snatch the pile of papers from her warm, sweaty little hands. I turn and grab Jack's and Brent's homework from them and I run.

'Oi!' Brent calls.

'What're you doing?' Jack shouts.

'Where's my kiss?' Stella screams.

I keep running and I don't turn back. *'I'll do the homework. Ha! How you like them apples? You're out of a job, Holling! I'm never kissing you again.'*

I run all the way to the bus, fly past Mrs Hamilton and leap on, just as the door is closing. I slide into the front seat and the bus moves off. I peer out through the dirty window at the three angry, twisted faces of

Jack, Brent and Stella, and I am happier than I've ever been in my life. For once, the good guy won. I outsmarted Stella Holling. I am a legend.

I wave to Stella, Brent and Jack. The bus turns and they are gone.

I look around to see if anyone else saw what just happened. No one seems that interested, which is a bit disappointing.

I look down at the heavy pile of homework in my lap. I flick through the 20 or 25 homework sheets. Oh, well, at least I don't have to kiss Stella.

In the past seven minutes I have gone from complaining about my homework to having no homework to having 25 people's homework to do from now until the end of time.

MY HOMEWORK:

BEFORE   AFTER

This makes me feel like not such a legend.
Twenty-five homework sheets. What was I
thinking?

Cars and houses and shops stream by
outside the window. My throat clamps up and
my face feels a bit tingly. What have I done?

I mean, Stella's not *that* bad.

And the red frog residue actually did smell
quite nice.

If I hurry back, I wonder if she'll still be
there? I wonder if she'll still kiss me.

The bus pulls up at the first stop and, without thinking, I jump off and start walking quickly back towards school.

'Hey, Tom. What are you doing?' a voice calls.

'Huh?' I turn. It's Sasha, the cutest and smartest girl in Australia. She has jumped off the bus behind me. She looks so beautiful in the orangey glow of afternoon sun that I can't speak.

'I'm going to my mum's work. Where are you going?' she asks.

'Um . . .' I try to think of a polite way to tell my future wife that I'm heading back to school to kiss another girl who I despise so that she'll do my homework.

It's a tricky situation.

I look down at the pile of papers in my

hand. 'Just . . . home,' I say, 'to do a bit of homework.'

'Oh, cool. I'm doing homework, too! I'm so glad you haven't been tempted to get involved in Stella's homework scam. I mean, what kind of idiot would fall for something like that?'

DR BENT

Ripping out five of my teeth seemed like such a good idea at the time, back when all that tooth fairy cash was rolling in. Jack and I were rich beyond our wildest dreams. We had rainbow Paddle Pops every lunchtime for two months.

Now, as I stand in the rain in front of a broken, molar-shaped, flickering-fluoro sign that reads 'Budget Dentistry', I'm not so sure. It seems that my mother will stop at nothing to save money. I thought pulling into a McDonald's car park on our trip to Sydney and feeding us egg-and-lettuce sandwiches was bad. Now she's risking the health and welfare of her own child.

I look down the cracked, moss-covered concrete path. It slithers through a dark forest to a timber house of peeling paint the colour of hot English mustard.

'C'mon,' Mum says. 'We're late.' She charges down the path, her high heels slipping from beneath her. She shoots out her hand and just manages to grab the rusty railing and save herself.

I hear the high-pitched zzzzzzzzz of the drill, and ice-cold fear whistles through me.

'Mum, please!'

'Don't be a sook, Tom. If you hadn't . . .' She starts on another rave about the stupidity of ripping out my own teeth. I mean, how was I supposed to know which were my baby teeth and which were my adult teeth?

'Come. Now.' She turns and slips on the mossy path again, falling right on her backside this time, scrambling to her feet and glaring at me through the gloom.

I follow – walking and sliding, slipping and skating – along the steep, winding concrete snake. As I reach the bottom of the path there's a bloodcurdling shriek from inside the surgery, and I stop dead in my tracks.

The house looms over me. It looks even more run-down than it did from the top gate. The windows are boarded up and the gutters are overflowing with leaves.

Mum knocks on the front door and waits.

'This place looks haunted,' I whisper,

walking slowly up the rotting front stairs.

'Maybe he's not a dentist. Maybe he's a psycho. Maybe he eats kids. Maybe–'

'Hello?' She pushes the door open. It creaks the way doors on creepy houses always do.

We step inside a wide, dark hallway. Another toe-curling scream chokes the air. It's a grown man, I think.

'Can we please just go to another dentist?' I whisper. 'I'll pay for it out of my own –'

'Hello-o!' Mum calls again into the darkness. This time the drill falls silent and the man's screams die.

A door opens on the right and a figure appears. He wears a bright headlamp, blinding us with its beam and lighting up dozens of animals' heads staring down at us from the dark timber walls. There is a wild boar with yellow tusks and two glassy-eyed foxes, a particularly devilish Tasmanian devil and many, many more. Each animal has its teeth bared in a permanent snarl.

'The art of taxidermy – just a little hobby,' says the dentist. He is hunched, with a shock of orange hair and a rattish, thin-lipped smile. Two twisted front teeth poke from his mouth towards us, as though *he* is one of the mounted animals.

'Welcome!' he says. 'I'm Dr Randalph Bent. You must be Tom Weekly.'

DENTISTS with bad teeth concern ME.

Another man emerges from the doorway behind Bent. The man's face is white and swollen up like a baseball mitt. He looks as though he's been to war, like he's seen and felt things that no human should.

'That'll be 27 dollars for today, Mr Francis,' Dr Bent says, pulling an old-fashioned credit card machine from the pocket of his blood-spattered dentist's jacket. My mother does not seem to see the blood. She only hears the price. No dentist has ever charged just 27 dollars for their services.

'Put some ice on it, and remember
Dr Bent's golden rule: "Don't be a baby."'
He laughs and hands the man his card and
receipt. 'Next victim!'

Mum grabs me by the elbow and steers me
towards the open door.

'Mum!' I hiss in a razor-sharp whisper, but
she ignores it, pushing me inside.

It does not look like a regular dentist's
surgery. There are no diplomas or certificates
on the walls. No metal trays with shiny silver
tools. There is no TV on the ceiling showing
gazelles galloping across the savanna to help
take the patient's mind off the pain. It's more
like . . . a kitchen. Dr Bent's surgery is an old
kitchen.

There's a single, buzzing fluorescent
tube overhead and a dirty, yellow tiled floor.

There's a kitchen sink and an empty space where a dishwasher once was. There's an old fridge with the cord unplugged and the door hanging open. It is filled with dental supplies – tubes and needles, pastes and scalpels.

My eyes settle on the dentist's chair in the middle of the room. Or maybe its eyes settle on me. I'm not sure which. I know that sounds strange, but the chair seems to be watching me. It's not a nice, modern, electric reclining chair like a normal dentist might have.

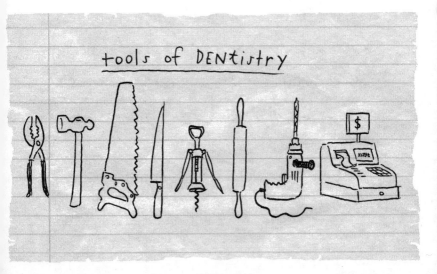

tools of DENtistry

It is old with poo-brown peeling leather. It is shaped like the head of an octopus – narrow at the seat and ballooning to a large, round backrest. Its eyes are two leather buttons positioned near the top of the head, and its arms look meaty and alive.

'Now, how may I help you?' Bent asks.

'Yesterday he removed one of his own adult teeth,' Mum says, her jaw clenched. 'This one.' She hands him the tooth wrapped in tissue.

Bent slowly unwraps it, turns it over and pokes at it with a dirty fingernail. 'Hmmm, self-extraction with pliers . . . I admire your technique.' He waves a hand towards the chair. 'Sit.'

I look at the chair. It looks at me. I will never, in my life, sit in that thing.

Dr Bent wraps his arm firmly around my shoulders and leads me to it. 'Don't be afraid. Betty won't bite.'

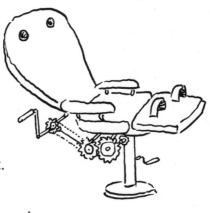

the CHAIR of death
(it's watching me!)

He presses me firmly into the chair and snaps on a blinding white light. I shield my eyes. Bent cranks a winding handle on the side of the chair. Cogs turn and the back reclines. Springs stretch and pop, and I find myself staring at the ceiling. I go to sit up but the arms of the chair fold in, clutching me tight. Metal clamps lock my legs.

'Just a precaution,' he says. 'Little ones can be jittery when they visit Dr Bent for the first time.'

'Mum?' I call.

She is sitting on a plastic chair to my right, chewing her nails.

'Just . . . do what the nice man says,' she tells me in a singsong voice.

'That's right. Be a big boy,' Bent says. 'Mummy just wants what's best for you.' A dark cloud seems to pass behind his eyes and he bares his fangs. 'Open up!'

He leans over me, panting death breath, grinning with the most terrifying teeth I have ever seen on a human being. (I was once spat on by an alpaca at a wildlife park. Its teeth were slightly worse.) Dr Bent's twisted fangs are pockmarked with decay. They reach out to me, like a 3D horror movie.

I reel back in the chair and go to shout 'Help!', but the second I open my mouth he jams a plastic wedge in. I bite down but I can't close my mouth.

'Let's have a little looky, shall we?' He peers deep into my gob. I can see him in close-up now, the whiteheads on his cheeks look ready to pop. Hundreds of long silver hairs sprout from each nostril. His dull, green eyes roil with menace. He scratches at my teeth with a sharp tool and pokes it deep into my gum where the tooth once was, making me yelp.

He turns to my mother. 'Okay then, we're going to make an incision in the gum, drill down into the jaw bone and screw in a steel rod. We'll pop the tooth back in and it'll be good as new.'

I turn to Mum, eyes wide. Surely she can't sit by and watch this maniac slice me up.

'I'm sorry to ask, but . . .' she begins. Oh, I love my mum so much. She's going to save me. I will never be rude to her again. I'll unpack the dishwasher tomorrow morning without her even making me. I'll stop stuffing my dirty clothes back in the drawer with all the clean ones. I'll brush my teeth every now and then. I'll – 'It sounds expensive. Do you know how much it might cost?'

tHis
Shouldn't
HURT
a bit.

Bent grins and takes a small calculator from his jacket pocket. He stabs at the numbers.

'It's your first visit, so why don't we make it an introductory offer of . . . 12 dollars and 50 cents.'

'What?!' I scream through the plastic wedge, but it comes out as 'Yacht?!'

My mother smiles and blushes. 'Thank you, doctor.'

Is she *insane*? This man isn't a doctor. He operates out of a kitchen. He's a butcher.

'Take a seat in the hall and Tom and I will get down to business.'

'Ugh-ugh!' I say, which means, 'Uh-uh.'

Mum stands, hesitating. She looks nervous but forces a smile. 'You be good.' She disappears into the hallway.

Bent clicks the door shut behind her and walks slowly towards me. He pulls on two grubby plastic gloves and holds up a drill. Not a dentist's drill, but a Black & Decker cordless drill like Pop had in his shed. It has sawdust and blood spattered all over it.

I spring my jaw wide and cough the plastic wedge out of my mouth. 'What are you doing?'

'The jaw is the hardest bone in the human body. Sometimes we need something with a little more *oomph* to get through it.' He revs the drill twice with his trigger finger.

'Aren't you going to numb the gum first?' I ask.

'Anaesthetic is for sissies,' he says. He lowers his voice to a whisper. 'Besides, I'm not legally allowed to administer it since I was thrown out of the Association for using horse tranquillisers on humans. And anyway, you're a strong boy. You'll be fine.' He revs the drill engine once more.

'What Association?'

'Please direct all queries to my assistant, Lucinda,' Bent says. 'We must get on.'

I look around the room but there is no assistant.

'Lucinda!' he calls. He puts two fingers in his mouth and whistles, which is a pretty rude way to call your assistant, if you ask me.

A flap at the bottom of the surgery door flips open and a small, grey, vicious-looking dog with fluffy ears darts into the room.

'Ah, Lucinda, deal with Mr Weekly's queries, will you?' Lucinda jumps onto the arm of the chair and then onto my chest, barking, growling, drooling and baring her teeth in my face.

Seeing the fear in my eyes, Bent says, 'No questions? Thank you, Lucinda.' The dog jumps down and sits at his feet.

'Is everything okay in there?' Mum asks.

'No!' I go to say, but Bent speaks over the top of me.

'Hunky dory!' he yells, and jams the wedge back in my mouth.

I try to break free but the arms of the chair hug me tighter. Its fingers grip my wrists.

'Ju-ust hold still,' he says, lowering the drill into my trap. 'This won't hurt a bit. Well, maybe just a *pinch*.'

I try to turn my head, but two padded restraints slide up out of the chair to prevent me. I try to move my arms and legs, but they are locked in hard. I try to close my mouth, but it's wedged open. I can't

believe my mother's bargain-hunting has
led to this.

The drill bit is inside my mouth now,
whirring and zizzing faster and faster.
It touches my jawbone, my skull explodes
with high-voltage pain, and I feel a rush of
superhuman strength. My arms strain at the
shackles. Veins appear. Nothing can hold
me down. I slip my skinny left arm out of
the clamp, reach up and grab his overgrown
nose hair between my thumb and forefinger,
and pull down hard. Bent squeals like a baby.
Tears shoot from his eyes, so I pull harder.
He rips his head back, banging his head
on the lamp, and falls to the floor. I'm left
clutching a handful of silver nose hair.

Bent's assistant, Lucinda, barks like a wild
thing.

Mum knocks on the door, rattling the handle. 'Tom, what's going on? Dr Bent?'

I strain and eventually squeeze my other arm from the clutches of the world's most evil dentist's chair. I kick hard at the leg clamps over and over again, then pry them open with my fingers. I leap from the chair and bolt for the door.

'Noooooo!' Bent shouts, jumping to his feet. Lucinda flies across the room after me, snapping at my heels. I grab an unlabelled body part in a pickle jar and hurl it at her. The jar explodes and Lucinda yelps.

I tear open the door and catapult myself into the hallway.

'Tom!' Mum says, but I run right past her.

'Get back here, you ungrateful pig of a boy!' Bent demands.

Lucinda, Bent and Mum
chase me up the hall, but
I'm too fast. They don't
have a hope. I run down
the wide, dark corridor,
past the parade of long-dead
animals. I pull open the front door and leap
down the five stairs in a single bound. I am
flying through the air and I am free. I will
never set foot inside Budget Dentistry again.
I am Tom Weekly, master of my own dentistry.
I mean destiny.

I land and the second my foot makes
contact with the path I feel it slip from
beneath me. But it's okay – my cat-like
reflexes will kick in and I'll save myself.
I always do. The wet path, carpeted in soft,
green moss, is speeding towards my face,

and I am now suspicious that my hands will not save me before my head makes contact with the – SLAM!

'Are you okay?!' Mum asks. She rolls me over and I look up at her. Raindrops fall through the trees and into my eyes. 'Oh no,' she whispers.

I touch my fingers to the roaring doughnut of pain that is my mouth. So smooth and wet. I sit up and see two small white pebbles embedded in the moss on the path. I reach out with a shaky hand and pluck the pebbles from the bright-green carpet. I rest them in the palm of my left hand.

Not pebbles.

My front teeth.

They are slick with dirt and blood and moss.

I slowly turn to Mum.

She growls like a beast, and I know what she's thinking: even at Budget Dentistry, this is going to cost a bit.

Over her shoulder Dr Bent gives me a look of crazed joy. He revs the cordless Black & Decker drill and snaps on his goggles. 'I'll do this one for free.'

WORST. DENTIST. EVER.

I'm not the only one with a dentist horror story. I've been speaking to kids in my class, and they told me things that will set the dental industry's relationship with children back 40 years.

* 'I got a needle through my tongue.'
  – Montana

* 'I had my gums lasered and they turned black.' – Natasha

* 'I nearly had my tongue sucked off by the sucker.' – Alana

* 'He had a tray of rotting teeth on the bench right next to my chair.' – Lilya

* 'The dentist went to the toilet in the middle of my appointment. It was right

next door, and I could hear that he didn't wash his hands. Then he stuck his fingers back in my mouth.' – Jaala

* 'I had to get five teeth ripped out in one sitting, with six needles for every tooth removed.' – Nick

* 'The trainee dentist took out my tooth. He accidentally dropped it and I swallowed it.' – Xavier

* 'The dentist got my lip stuck underneath my braces. Then he ripped my lip.' – Nat

* 'He sneezed a booger onto my face.' – Thomas

* 'He used a dirty mouth sponge on me.' – Kai

* 'I couldn't feel the left side of my face. I tried to eat something when I got home and I bit off the side of my tongue.' – Chris

Got your own weird or freaky dentist story?
I want to hear it at thetomweekly@gmail.com

REVENGE OF THE NITS
(PART ONE)

Head lice scuttle across the bright, white scalp like lobsters on the ocean floor. They sink their bloodsucking tubes into Lewis's skin and grow plump, turning a rusty orange colour; then they scurry on. You have not lived until you've seen head lice grazing on a scalp in close-up through a macro lens.

'Quiet on set . . . camera rolling. And . . . action!' I whisper.

47

Jack pours my nan's spaghetti sauce in a straight line from the back of Lewis's hair, over his ear to his forehead. I watch the action unfold on the camera's flip-screen. Hundreds of head lice are stopped in their tracks. Others are blown off their feet by the force of the sauce. A few manage to vanish into the undergrowth. In our movie, this attack is a bombing raid by an alien race called the Zoronites, using radioactive red sludge mined from deep underground on their home planet, Zoron.

'And cut!' I say. 'That was awesome.'

'Play it back!' Jack demands.

We are in Lewis's bedroom. Lewis is one of my best friends, and he just happens to have the worst case of nits in world history. He's had nits so long that he sees them as

his pets. He says they 'talk' to him (which makes me worry about his mental health). He's kindly letting us use his head as a set to shoot our disaster movie for Media class. The assignment was to make a short film about bullying. But that seemed kind of boring. And we figure nits have been pushed around, poisoned, combed out and squished to death by humans for tens of thousands of years, so our Nits vs Aliens story is a

heart-warming call for the fairer treatment
of head lice and millions of other bugs
and parasites that call our bodies home.
Or that's what we're telling Miss Norrish
anyway. Really, we just want to make a cool
alien movie.

Lewis is kneeling on a sheet of black plastic
we laid out on the carpet. The camera is on a
tripod, hovering over him.

I show Jack the footage and he whoops
with joy.

'One more shot,' I say. 'Just for good luck.'

'Do we have to?' Lewis groans. 'You didn't
hurt any of them, did you?'

'No,' I say. 'All safe and sound.'

I feel bad saying this because, I'm afraid,
insects *have* been harmed in the making of
this motion picture.

Lewis scratches his head where the sauce landed.

'Don't!' I tell him. 'It has to look the same in the next shot. It's called "continuity". I'm going in for a close-up of the nits' reactions.'

'Sorry, it's just kind of itchy,' Lewis says.

'*Kind of* itchy?' Jack laughs. 'That's funny. *Kind of* itchy.'

'What?' Lewis asks.

'That's like saying Pluto is *kind of* far away,' Jack says. 'Or that Tom's bum is *kind of* smelly. Or that Madonna is *kind of* old. You have more nits than everyone in our school put together – everyone in *every* school put together.' Lewis looks hurt. Jack doesn't notice. 'You need to go to the doctor. You need to go to the zoo. You *are* the zoo!'

Lewis looks like he is about to punch Jack in the nose. I've had to stop them from fighting a few times during our two-hour shoot.

'Let's just do this last shot and finish up,' I tell them. 'We've got to start editing if we want to hand it in tomorrow. Quiet on set . . . camera rolling. And . . . action!'

We do it all again. Jack starts pouring a single line of sauce but, halfway, I see a wicked grin creep across his face and he dumps the entire contents of the jar onto Lewis's head, causing mass nit destruction. Lewis's wild blond 'fro flattens to his head. Sauce drips down his face and into his ears.

'And . . . cut!' I say.

'What was *that*?' Lewis screams, standing and knocking the tripod over. I manage to catch it before the camera hits the floor.

Lewis lunges at Jack. Jack backs off. My arm shoots out to stop Lewis, but I'm not quick enough. He goes for Jack's throat.

I grab the back of Lewis's shirt and pull on it like reins. Jack points at Lewis's hair. 'Dude, what's happening to your head?'

'Grrrrrrrr!' Lewis bares his teeth and his eyes bulge like an angry marsupial.

'Seriously! Take a look,' Jack says.

I look closely at the back of Lewis's head.

I see lumps. Lots of lumps. Dozens, maybe hundreds of them, each one about the size of a marble. They're writing and

Nan's tomato sauce

wriggling beneath Lewis's sauce-coated hair. I let go of Lewis's shirt and step back. 'You better go look in the mirror.'

Lewis goes to his wardrobe door, looks closely at his scalp, screams and drops to the floor.

'Is he dead?' Jack asks.

'No, he fainted, you idiot!' I watch Lewis carefully. 'At least I think he fainted . . .'

I lean down and place my hand on Lewis's chest. It moves up and down, so I grab the camera and start filming as a few claws emerge from beneath the saucy hair blanket. A very large nit scuttles down Lewis's face and onto his chest. Then another and another and another. They scatter onto the floor. They are at least the size of my thumb now. I stare into one of the nits' eyes, and it almost looks intelligent. Lewis's head is a churning sea of lice claws, jaws and pincers.

'It's the sauce,' Jack says. 'What's in it?'

'How am I supposed to know?' I say. 'Nan says it's her "secret recipe". It tastes disgusting.'

I keep filming. It is the most disturbing thing I have ever seen on a camera screen. Even more disgusting than the time I filmed my sister Tanya sleeping so that I could prove to her that she snores when she drinks too much milk.

A head louse runs over Jack's foot, and he squeals and flicks it off. The louse flies through the air with a very faint scream and slams, headfirst, into Lewis's bedroom wall. It explodes and red and green goo drips down towards the carpet.

Jack splats three or four more head lice into the carpet. There are a hundred or so nits scurrying across the floor now.

'Let's go!' Jack shouts.

'What about Lewis?'

'What *about* Lewis?' he asks. 'They're *his* nits. Let's save ourselves.'

'Grab his feet,' I tell Jack. I unclip the camera from the tripod and hang it around my neck, still filming. I shove my hands under Lewis's armpits. There is an almost electric connection when we touch. Nits surge from Lewis's body, up my arms and onto my shoulders. I feel them nibble at the nape of my neck and I flick off as many as I can. Jack backs towards the door.

'Grab his *feet*!' I scream. 'We've got to wash the sauce off him.' I'm panicking because there are hundreds of nits blooming from Lewis's scalp now. Lewis's body is covered with them and, now, so am I. I think I read somewhere that head lice won't live anywhere south of your eyebrows. I think they're trying to get to my head.

The ones on the floor are still covered in sauce, and they just seem to get bigger and bigger and bigger. Some of them are the size of small guinea pigs now.

Jack stomps across the room, splatting huge head lice beneath his size six shoes. The nits erupt, spraying the carpet with meaty head lice chunks. Jack grabs Lewis's legs and lifts. We move quickly across to the bedroom door. I take one last look back. The floor is heaving with thousands of mini-beasts, growing larger by the second, scurrying in every direction. They follow us as we move out the door, like they can smell the delicious blood pumping through our veins.

We walk as quickly as we can down the hall and into the bathroom. I kick the door closed, crushing a pair of nits between the door and frame.

'Sorry,' I say to them. Lewis would be very upset if he had seen that. He loves his pets. I kick the door again and it clicks closed, snapping one of the bigger nits in two.

'Quick, wash him off!' I tell Jack.

We drop Lewis into the bath and Jack leaps in after him, clawing at his own neck, face and head. He squeals like a piglet, flicking off 30 or 40 thumb-sized nits.

I flip on the tap and water gushes over Lewis's scalp. I start to scrub the sauce and nits out of his hair. It's like massaging a nest of tarantulas. I have to look away in order to keep the baked bean toastie that I had for afternoon tea down. Jack jumps out of the bath when he sees the plump head lobsters raining down from Lewis's head.

The water splashing Lewis's face starts to wake him, but I force his head back under the tap until I can scrape most of the sauce and nits off. The camera around my neck still has the red record light on, and it's pointing right at Lewis. I pray that it's in focus and capturing this disaster as it unfolds. Somewhere, in the back of my mind, I hear the words, 'Academy Award-winning filmmaker, Tom Weekly.'

'Lemme up,' Lewis says groggily, like a boxer pulling himself up off the mat.

Most of the nits have been prised from his scalp, so I help him out of the tub. The lice try to climb up the side of the bath, but it's too slippery. I rip the little bloodsuckers off my arms and throw them in with the others. Then I notice something amazing. The nits that have been hit by the water, that have had the sauce washed off, have shrunk. They are so small they're being washed down the plughole. Lots of them are now the size of regular nits.

'What happened?' Lewis asks.

'The sauce,' I tell him. 'There's something in it. The longer the sauce is on them, the bigger they grow. They're like gremlins.'

There is a loud gnawing sound. Lewis and I both turn to see 15 to 20 head louse snouts chewing on the bottom of the door. The lice that these noses belong to must be as big as

possums, or maybe
even wombats now.
They are making an
increasingly large pile
of sawdust and wood
chips on the floor.

'They'll eat us
alive,' Jack says.
'We need weapons.'

'Water,' I say.
'We need to spray
them.'

I turn to the shower
and twist the tap on, but it's such a gentle
spray – it'll never make it to the door.

'The sink tap!' I say to Jack and he twists it
on, using his thumb to direct the water, but
the spray only reaches halfway to the door.

So Jack opens the cupboard beneath the sink and pulls out rolls of toilet paper and bars of soap. 'There's no bucket,' he says. Then he holds up a green bottle of conditioner, the same brand Mum uses to get rid of my nits.

'NO!' Lewis says.

'YES!' Jack replies. He goes to the door and sprays the conditioner all over the louse snouts. They pull back and squeal, momentarily stunned, but then they take to the door with even greater gusto.

Jack returns to the cupboard, grabs the mould cleaner and starts to squirt, but Lewis knocks it out of his hand.

'What're you doing, nit boy?' Jack snips.

'We don't hurt them,' Lewis says firmly. And Lewis doesn't speak firmly very often. 'No one lays another foot or finger on my nits, got it?' We both glance down at Jack's sneaker, which is spattered with red and green guts.

Jack swallows hard. You can tell he's scared of Lewis's quiet, fiery determination. The lice are seriously woodchipping the door now. The left-hand side has a giant bite out of it.

Jack looks around frantically. 'The window,' he says.

High over the bath there's a very small window, about 40 centimetres wide and 30 centimetres high. It would be big enough for Lewis, maybe Jack, but I doubt whether it'll be big enough for my gigantic head.

There is an explosion of timber and dozens of pit-bull-terrier-sized head lice explode through the door. They are covered in Nan's tomato sauce and they look angry, rabid and hungry for human blood.

Jack and I scream 'GO!' and scramble for the window. While I give Jack a boost, Lewis just stands there, rubbing his hands together as the lice charge towards him, their feet slipping on the tiles.

'What're you doing, you maniac?' I shout.

Jack is already halfway out the window. The nits are seconds from taking Lewis down.

'I'll talk to them,' Lewis says. 'I understand them. They'll listen to me.'

I grab him by the collar and drag him up onto the edge of the bath. As soon as Jack's feet disappear, I boost Lewis up to the window. 'Wait!' he protests. 'Let me talk –' As his head disappears outside, a murderous mutant louse sinks its fine, jagged teeth deep into my ankle.

Turn to page 151 to see what happens next!

Fig I

louse

Fig II

house

Fig III

louse eAts
house

SCAB COLLECTION

I have the most epic collection of scabs, but I've never shown it to anyone. I've always been worried that someone will break into my house, steal the collection and sell the individual scabs on eBay for thousands. But I found an old safe when we went to the dump last weekend. That's where I keep my collection now, so there's no chance of anyone stealing it. Unless they take the whole safe. It's not very heavy. And the door doesn't close because the lock is busted.

But anyway . . . I welcome you to peruse my priceless collection of crispy, wafer-thin blood-biscuits. They each have a name. Naming scabs is one of the most fun things in the world. It's like cloud-gazing, trying to work out what each scab looks like and then – BOOM! – it hits you: 'Taylor Swift', or 'double-decker bus', or 'killer magpie driving its beak through my skull'.

So, here it is . . . the world premiere of Tom Weekly's Epic Scab Collection. Enjoy!

TOM WEEKLY's
˙'EPIC˙' SCAB COLLECTION

(THE SMITHSONIAN Institute
will BUY this ONE day)

THE SPONGE
BoB

amphibious
Landing
crAft

Stella's
lips

The SubMARine

Eiffel
TOWER
(or Rocket
ship!)

the
fiG

Exploding
VOLCANO

TIME
travel
machiNe

potato
(or Asteroid)
(or football)
(or Jack's
brain)

LIGHT
bulb

Intergalactic SWORD (or stick)

Unicorn

The Tarantula

The GREAT WHITE

LEWIS's Head

T-rex

The CHICKEN

I can't decide what this is BUT it's cool

LASER ray gun

LOCH NeSS Monster

World's FASTEST Car (or weird carrot)

AnacoNDa

'DON'T SIT WHERE YOU KNIT'

Here's a true tale by one of my friends, Indigo.
She's twelve years old, lives in Canberra,
and her story was so good I had to include it
in my book.

'Get in the car!' Mum shouted.

She was not in her best mood. I flung my knitting bag, containing my double-pointed sock-knitting needles, through the car door and leaped in after it. Onto my knitting bag!

My bum hurt, but I didn't make a sound until I looked behind me and saw one of my needles sticking out of my left buttock.

I screamed until Mum raced out to the car.
Then *she* screamed. I kind of wished she would
do something to help instead of screaming.
I really wasn't up for having a knitting needle
poking out of my bum, and a headache.

Mum started to pull. I could feel my bum
skin holding on tight. We both knew it wasn't
about to hand over that needle. So Mum
slammed the door, jumped
into the front seat and sped
down to the Medical
Centre. I had to face the
rear window with my
backside in the air.
When we arrived,
I struggled to get
out of the car,
bottom first.

Ah-ha! That's where I left my knitting NEEDLE!

I waddled into the waiting room with my bum sticking out behind me like Donald Duck. My face was red and blotchy. It does that when I cry. An old lady with a bandaged nose stared at me. Her mouth hung open wide enough to stuff a pair of socks in. A boy with a broken arm tried to nudge his sister to get her to look at me. He didn't have much control over his arm and he missed, hitting a man with long red hair instead. The redhead stared at me for far longer than was polite and then began to laugh! When he saw me looking, he pulled his newspaper over his face and continued to shake with laughter.

I didn't have to wait, not that I could have sat down anyway. No one complained about me jumping the queue. The doctor thought the needle may have hit a nerve. He gave me a local anaesthetic and cut a slit right next to the needle to investigate. I could actually feel him slicing into my bum. He discovered that the needle wasn't touching the nerve, but it was millimetres away. If I was just a kilogram heavier . . .

I went home that day with four stitches in my bum and a bloody, double-pointed knitting needle. We measured how far it went in. SEVEN AND A HALF CENTIMETRES!

My bum throbs just thinking about it. My knitting teacher said that I could keep that set of needles.

DEATH BY CLOWN

'Hey Tom.'

Oh no.

It's her.

On the phone.

Talking to me, Tom Weekly.

Why would she want to talk to me? I'm so nervous I want to throw up. This is the worst day of my life. I'm –

'Tom?'

'Yeah?'

Sasha. The cutest and smartest girl in Australia.

'Are you okay?' she asks.

What do you say to someone with eyes like blue sky, a voice like a mango smoothie and fresh, minty breath like an Arctic breeze? Not that I can smell it right now, but I can imagine it. So minty.

'Tom?'

She sounds a bit annoyed. I can't mess this up. I always mess things up with Sasha. Like the time I told her I was attacked by a giant feral guinea pig, who bit off my toe. Why am I such a –

'We've got a spare front-row ticket to the circus tonight because my brother has to go to karate and Thalia and Leilani and Sophie and Brittany are busy. So do you want to come?'

Circus.

'Tom?'

'Huh?'

'I'm asking you to the circus.'

'Um . . .' I'm sweating. I try to tell myself that it's just because Sasha has called my house for  the first time in our long on-again, off-again relationship. But I know that's not it.

'Mum's calling me,' Sasha says. 'I've got to get ready. Do you want to come or not, Tom?'

My head froths with fear and panic – white-faced, red-nosed, fuzzy-haired, polka-dotted panic. But this is Sasha, my kryptonite.

'Yes,' I whisper.

'"Yes" you'll come?'

'Yes,' I say again, slightly louder, my voice breaking in an awkward way.

'Great,' she says. Although she doesn't sound so sure now. 'We'll pick you up in fifteen minutes.'

'Fifteen,' I repeat.

'See you soon.' Sasha hangs up.

'I'm dead,' I say to the beeping phone line. I have front-row seats to my own death.

I press 'End' and place the phone on the kitchen bench. I have never admitted this to anyone other than my mother, but I have a morbid fear of clowns. And when I say 'morbid', I mean 'psychologically unhealthy'. And when I say 'psychologically unhealthy', I mean they freak me out. I can't be near them. But, in everyday life, that's fine. I just avoid little kids' birthday parties, certain fast food outlets . . . and circuses. I have my coulrophobia (fear of clowns) under control.

Or at least I thought I did. Until about 17 seconds ago.

Mum comes into the kitchen, takes a bag of baby peas from the freezer and pours them into boiling water on the stove. 'What's wrong?' she asks.

'Sasha,' I say.

'What about her?'

'She asked me out,' I say.

'Really! That's great. I think you're going to marry her one day.'

'No,' I say.

'You're not going to marry her?'

'No. Circus.'

'You're not going to marry her at the circus?'

'She asked me to go to the circus. In 15 minutes.'

'Oh dear,' she says. 'Did you say no?'

I shake my head.

'Well, it's probably about time you got over it. You were three years old, Tom.'

I think back to the painting that Mum did. She hung it on the wall over my bed on the night of my third birthday. It still smelt like oil paint. I don't think it ever really dried. The picture was of a tall, skinny clown in a blue polka-dot suit, red bow tie, fedora hat and evil diamond eyes.

Me? CrEEPy?

Every night from the age of three till I finally ripped the painting down when I was eight, he would slither out over the frame and into my bedroom. Some nights he would drop juggling balls onto my head for hours. Or strum an out-of-tune ukulele till four in the morning. Or sit right next to my ear and squeakily twist balloons into the shapes of werewolves, llamas and baboons.

I try to shake the clown from my thoughts, but there's no way out of this. Girls like Sasha don't just call up every night and ask guys like me to go out with them. My pop always said, 'Never look a gift horse in the mouth.' I never knew what he meant. But maybe this is it – not that Sasha is a horse. Although she does have kind of a long face and she sometimes has sliced apples for morning tea.

TOM WEEKLY'S Guide to clown Balloon animals

 werewolf

MONGOLiaN
Death worm

 Chupacabra
(they're freaky
- look it up!)

The BEAST
of Bodmin MOOR

MothMan
(they EAT your
organs!)

 Blood-sucking
poodle

What if I'd said no and she asked some other guy like Zane Smithers? They would start going out together. They would end up getting married and having three kids and a labradoodle and a house overlooking the ocean with secret passages and revolving bookcases. All because I'd said no to going to the circus.

Over my dead body will I let that happen.

Dead body.

Mine.

The lights go down. Excitement swells – cheers and whistles and howls. Five hundred excited people are seated around the circus ring under the big top. Correction: 499 excited, one terrified.

'What are you excited to see?' Sasha asks, popping a piece of purple popcorn into her mouth. 'I love the tightrope and the hula hoops, but I can't wait for the clowns. They're so funny. My favourite clown is . . .'

I tune out. Even the mention of the word 'clown' dries out my tongue and dampens my armpits. I squinch my eyes closed. I should be happy. I'm sitting next to Sasha. I can smell her minty breath, hear her mango smoothie voice, and our knees even touched a few minutes ago.

Yet I am filled with dread. The clown from the painting over my bed slithers back into my mind. Wherever I would go in my bedroom his eyes would follow. Sometimes I'd feel him watching me in other rooms, too. And at school. Even on holidays at the beach. There's a phobia called anatidaephobia, which is the fear that – no matter where you are – a duck is watching you. Maybe that's what I have, except with clowns. No matter what I said, for years Mum wouldn't take the painting down. 'Don't be silly. Kids love clowns,' she would say. 'Don't you like my painting?'

BOOM!

There is an explosion and a burst of flame that sends shockwaves through the crowd. My heart leaps into my head. Ten trapeze artists swing down from the big top. Five let go and the other five catch them in midair. Water fountains erupt all around the ring. A long-haired motorbike stunt rider soars over a jump and comes to land in front of us. She skids to a stop on the sawdust floor, rips off her helmet and raises her hand for silence.

ANATIDAEPHOBIA

'Ladieeeees and gentlemennnnn! Welcome to Dingaling Brothers Circus, the most extraordinary display on Earth!'

'That's amazing,' Sasha says, squeezing my hand.

It is. For the next hour, we are dazzled by unbelievable magic, stunts and acrobatics. And you know what? Not a single clown. That is, until the lights go down after the human cannonball and I hear the honking sound of a cheap rubber horn. Every hair on my body stands to attention.

The lights snap on again. Not a slow fade but a violent snap.

A clown emerges from between the tall velvet curtains on the far side of the ring. He's driving a tiny, kid-sized fire truck, his knees up around his ears. He waves to the crowd and blows his horn over and over again. As he moves closer and closer, I start to realise who he is. He is not just any clown. His hair is black and he wears a blue polka-dot suit, a red bow tie and a fedora hat. He is the sweaty, demonic clown from my mother's painting.

I wet my pants. Not a lot, but definite leakage.

'I have to go to the toilet,' I tell Sasha, panicking. I stand and start to leave.

'Nooo, this is my favourite part. I love the clowns. Please stay.' She grabs my hand and pulls me back down. Clown-fear and Sasha-love battle to the death in my chest.

The crowd all around me is cracking up. As he zooms towards us I see that his truck has 'Giggles' written on the side. *Giggles the Clown*. He comes to a stop in front of us, his fire truck skidding in the sawdust. He falls out of the truck onto his face. The crowd erupts with laughter.

He stands, dusts himself off and looks directly at me.

He knows me.

He knows that I know that he knows me.

And he wants revenge for what I did to him.

Sweat stings my eyes. I slide down low in my chair.

Giggles motions to the crowd like he wants a helper. I slide down further in my seat, trying to become invisible. Giggles lowers his chin, glares at me through his thick brows, points and motions to me with one crooked, white-gloved finger.

Sasha claps wildly. 'Tom! It's you! He wants you!'

I can't get up.

'Just go!' Sasha says.

I shake my head, cross my arms, squinch my eyes shut again.

'Go on, young man!' says the grandma sitting to my right.

'How about you go, lady?' I snap.

'Get up, Tom!' says Sasha's dad. 'What's wrong with you?'

I shake my head. I have another flashback to the painting over my bed, the night he slipped out over the frame and tried to suffocate me with the world's unfunniest clown fart. It smelt like dead mice, ginger beer and cauliflower. I was drowning in it. I held my breath for almost two minutes before I could swim to the surface of that deathly stench. I wrestled him back into the picture frame and ripped the painting off the wall.

Every now and then you wish the Earth would open up a hole just big enough to jump through. TODAY is that day.

I dragged it outside in the dark of night and hid it in the shed behind the plastic tubs of camping gear and old tiles and tins of paint. Mum asked where the painting had gone, but I never, ever owned up to my crime. I thought that was the end of him, until tonight.

Someone yells, 'Boooo!' Someone else says, 'Come on, kid. Hurry up!'

When I still refuse to move, Sasha's dad jumps out of his seat, picks me up and puts me over his shoulder.

'No!' I struggle and pound my fists against his back to let me down, but he's too strong. He carries me into the ring. He dumps me on the ground next to Giggles, who takes me by the arm. Sasha's dad strides back to his seat to wild applause.

Giggles pulls something out of his pocket and holds it up to the crowd. He does not speak, just points and fake-smiles. It is a clown suit. From his other pocket he produces a bright orange wig. He turns to me with those bloodshot eyes of doom, oil paint dripping down his face. Spider webs and dead grass are tangled in the wig that pokes out from the edge of his fedora. He smells like our shed – lawnmower fuel and rat droppings. I want to run but he digs his long fingernails into the soft flesh of my upper arm. I look out at the crowd.

'Put it on!' they scream.

I look at Sasha. She's smiling at me with a face full of expectation. So I pull the stupid clown suit on. It is white with rainbow spots and a pink-and-orange ruff around the neck.

Giggles pulls the wig down hard on my head, then plants a kids' fire helmet on top. He slathers my face in white make-up using a paintbrush big enough to paint a house. He snaps a red nose on me and scrawls lipstick across my lips. The crowd loves every minute. He's a funny guy, Giggles.

He shoves me backwards into the small fire truck that he arrived in. My feet are hanging over the front because it's so small. There is a little steering wheel perched between my legs. Giggles holds up a large, silver, glittery box and pulls up an aerial. He flicks a switch and the fire truck takes off. Soon, the

I have OFFICIALLY died.

crowd is a blur. I am speeding around the ring with a demented clown at the controls. I am embarrassed and petrified, and hundreds of people are watching me. They start up a clap in time with the crazy circus music.

Giggles' sickly, black tongue squirms at the corner of his mouth as he stands in the centre of the ring, steering the truck with the remote. His eyes are narrow and he gleams with sweat. He throws an arm in the air and a thick wall of flame leaps from the floor right next to him.

Giggles turns the fire truck hard and it skids to a stop. I try to pull myself out of the truck, but it takes off again before I have a chance. I am heading directly towards the wall of fire. Surely this lunatic isn't going to drive a child through fire? There's no way I'll get through it without being toasted like a marshmallow.

The crowd seems to realise what is happening. They stop clapping as I speed towards the blaze.

My throat closes up. I'm only 20 metres from being burnt alive and I'm gaining speed. I can't jump out now – I'm going too fast. I grab the wheel and rip it to the right. The truck moves right but Giggles, with the remote control, steers me back towards the fire. I rip it to the left and Giggles steers me back again.

I can see the crowd behind him. They look worried, which worries me even more. People call out 'STOP!', but Giggles is hell-bent on killing me, I know it.

Tom Weekly does not go down without a fight. I decide to drive the truck right at him.

I will face my fear and take him down. I've had enough. It's Tom Weekly vs Giggles the Clown, and the Gigmeister is going down.

He stands just to the left of the wall of fire. As I twist the wheel, charging towards him, I see a flicker of fear in his red-rimmed eyes. The speeding fire truck is ten metres from both the flames and the world's most dastardly clown. He steers me towards the fire, and I steer back. He steers me towards the fire again, and I steer back. I'm five metres away and I can feel the terrible inferno. Giggles is hunched over the remote control and is not about to give in. Good, because neither am I. I am two metres from the fire and there is a very real chance that I am about to be barbecued. Crowd members run into the ring towards us. Sasha's dad is one of them.

TOM WEEKLY VS GIGGLES THE CLOWN

* THE CLOWN is GOING DOWN !

Now! I tear the wheel to the left and clamp it there with my hands and knees. I put every last shred of muscle and energy that I have into this.

The fire engine skids and feels like it's about to roll when the shiny silver bumper bar hits Giggles right in the shins. He screams, falls backwards, and his oversized clown shoes flip the truck up in an explosion of ladders and jingling bells. I am thrown out of the truck towards the devastating wall of fire. I hit the ground hard and flames lick my clown suit, setting my wig alight. My head is on fire, and I roll over and over to kill the flames. Someone from the crowd helps.

As soon as the flames are out, I look back. The truck has stopped dead, right on top of Giggles. His arms and legs are pinned beneath the vehicle. The remote control, aerial snapped, lies on the sawdust next to him.

Two clown paramedics run across the ring with a stretcher. Sasha and her dad reach me. I sit up. Sasha gives me a huge hug. In that moment, feeling the warmth and kindness of her, and the relief of knowing that I am alive, my coulrophobia seems to slip away.

I am no longer afraid of clowns.

Sasha holds my hand all the way home in the car.

'Goodnight, Tom,' she says when we pull up outside my house. She looks at me in a way she's never looked at me before. I gaze back.

'Alrighty then,' says her dad, switching on the car's interior light.

'Okay, g'night,' I say, climbing out of the car.

Sasha wipes steam from the back window and watches me as they drive off. I float up my front path on an air-biscuit of Sasha-love. I knock on the front door. Footsteps. The door opens. Mum screams when she sees me dressed as a lightly toasted clown.

'What are you wearing *that* for?'

'Long story,' I say, pushing past her.

'How did you go with the clowns?'

'Good. I mean not good. I'll tell you in the morning,' I say, heading down the hall.

I shut the bathroom door and rest my back against it. I sniff the hand that Sasha was holding. I can smell her popcorny goodness. I decide to never wash that hand again. I figure I'll put it in a plastic bag when I shower.

I look at myself in the mirror. I have saved my life, overcome my fear of clowns and won the girl of my dreams – all in one night. I straighten my burnt, orange wig and adjust my nose. I look kind of cool. Sasha loves clowns. Maybe that's why she looked at me that way?

I smile at the mirror, then I bare my teeth like I'm about to eat a small child. Then I smile sweetly again. It's fun to be a clown.

I squeeze the spurty flower stuck to my clown suit and water drips down the mirror, blurring my reflection.

I think back to Giggles being arrested and taken away in cuffs after receiving medical attention from the clown doctor. I guess Dingaling Brothers will probably be looking for someone to replace him. And for the first time in my life, I think I know what I want to be when I grow up.

MY CAT'S SO FAT . . .

I have to admit, we are pretty bad pet owners.
We feed our cat Gordon all the wrong things —
chicken necks, cheese fries, chocolate milk.
Mum just can't help but give him our leftovers.
He's a disgrace. Gordon's so fat . . .

* When he walks in front of the TV
  you miss the whole series.

* He doesn't eat sardines, he eats orcas.

I see
your PROBLEM.
YOUR cat is
REEALLLY
fat.

* He's got his own postcode.

* He sat on my foot this morning and broke three toes.

* His collar is the equator.

* When Frisbee – the poodle next door – went missing, the cops had Gordon X-rayed.

* The kennel charges us Large Dog rates when we go on holidays.

* Kings Bay Theatre Company wants him to play a wombat in their latest adaptation of a Jackie French book.

* When a fireman tried to rescue him from a tree, Gordon fell and crushed the fire truck.

* On Sunday afternoon he jumped on the trampoline and our neighbours, having a barbecue, complained he kept blocking out the sun.

* His milk saucer is an Olympic swimming pool.

My body is A temple.
A really round temple
WHEre you can eat pizza
and sleep all day.

* On Monday he ate a bird. Not that unusual for a cat. But this was a pelican.

* My star sign is Sagittarius. His is Doritos.

* When he was in the front yard yesterday, a calf from a nearby field thought Gordon was his mama and tried to drink his milk.

* He did a poo in the middle of our street and Kings Bay Shire Council had to send a bulldozer to remove it.

* He swished his tail and took out the mailman, two girls playing handball on the footpath and a ute.

* His furballs are so fat my mum thought he'd had kittens.

* When he runs around the house, people in Tokyo think there's been an earthquake.

* He's officially been named Earth's eighth continent: Gordonia.

* When he went to the beach, the local whale society thought they had discovered a new species and tried to drag him back out to sea.

Fungus the Bogeyman

I am crouched in the bushes across the road from Kings Bay Public Library. I have a copy of a book called *Fungus the Bogeyman* in my trembling left hand. The prickly native bush is scratching my left ear and I have a branch sticking into my bum cheek, but I dare not move.

Cars crisscross between me and the front door of the library. Right next to the door is the returns machine. It is a large, black square set into the wall like a bank ATM. It has a pulsing red digital eye that watches everything and a wide, greedy mouth that eats books. I have been thinking about this machine for five long years. Sometimes I imagine it to have yellow teeth and a disgusting, white tongue when its mouth opens, its dusty breath smelling of 10,000 old books.

Next to the returns machine is a sign in large letters:

SECURITY NOTICE:
THIS BUILDING IS UNDER
24-HOUR SURVEILLANCE.

Above the sign there is a security camera mounted on the wall, and I have reason to worry . . .

When I was six years old I borrowed *Fungus the Bogeyman* from the library, and I

have had it out ever since. Three weeks after I borrowed it, the first overdue notice came.

Then the second. And by the third notice, when my overdue fees were higher than the cost of the book, I decided I could never go back to the public library again. I hid the notices from Mum. For five long years, Fungus has lurked inside the trapdoor beneath my bedroom rug, shaking his boogery head at me, disgusted. *I* should be disgusted with Fungus and the 10,000 green boogers inside his nose but, instead, he is disgusted with me . . . Late fees are ten cents a day, so I currently owe $186.70.

But I really *want* to go to the library. They have great books and air conditioning and comfy chairs, and I've heard they give lollies and milkshakes to kids at book club. If I take back *Fungus* I'm scared to death of what the librarians will do to me, but the guilt is too much.

I've confessed my fears to Jack, and he thinks I'm overreacting, but what would Jack know about libraries? He's never been in one.

He breaks out in hives when he even looks at a book. He wouldn't even return *Fungus* for me.

I open the book. The first pages show the inside of Fungus the Bogeyman's nose – bright-green boogers in super-macro close-up. It makes me feel kind of sick. Not because I'm squeamish about boogers, but because boogers remind me of my crime and the money I owe.

If I just walked into a shop, opened the till, removed $186.70 and ran, they'd probably call the police, right? Well . . . that's pretty much what I've done. So here's my plan:

1. Get out of prickly Australian native bush.
2. Cross road.
3. Climb steps.
4. Deposit book in slot.

5. Slip around side of building and disappear into thick undergrowth behind library.

It's time I close this chapter of my life. Jack is probably right. I am overreacting. I am a professional overreactor. I need to have my imagination surgically removed.

Before I know it I've completed steps one to three. I'm two metres from the returns machine and being watched by that all-seeing eye. Any moment I'll trigger the face-recognition technology, or the barcode will trip an alarm, and it'll be the end of my time on the run.

I make it to the returns slot, scan the barcode, and the machine whirrs and whirrs and whirrs. *C'mon,* I urge. I look over my shoulder and there is a lady in a pink tracksuit standing behind me with an armful of novels. She smiles and I'm immediately suspicious – people don't just smile at each other in public for no reason.

The machine beeps and then its mouth starts to open. I brace myself, ready for it to taser me or deliver a devastating blast of knock-out gas before it sucks me into its mechanical belly. But it just continues to whirr. Finally, the digital display reads, 'Please Deposit Your Books Now.' I tentatively move my head towards the machine and sniff. It doesn't smell like 10,000 old books at all. It doesn't smell like anything. And it doesn't have teeth or a tongue. Just harmless mechanical rollers.

I kiss Fungus on the forehead and hope that the lady behind doesn't see me. I feed the book into the slot. The mouth closes, the machine stops whirring, the digital readout says, 'Thank You For Using Kings Bay Public Library', and it's over. Chapter closed.

I turn and grin at the lady with the stack of books. For the first time in five long years I have actually used the public library. I turn around to the street and drink in the sunshine and salty air. I'm a free man. The book is back. Maybe I could even come in next week and try using my card. Maybe they don't keep records that long. Maybe they'll welcome me back into the family.

An alarm sounds – loud, high-pitched and insistent – like a fire alarm. Red light flashes just above the returns machine. Just then, a white van mounts the kerb and skids to a stop on the footpath. It has a Kings Bay Public Library logo on the front and side.

I start to back up towards my escape route into the bush behind the library, just like I planned. Three librarians jump out of the side of the van.

'Stop right there!' one of them yells. She is the youngest, has her hair in a ponytail, wears sweat pants and looks like she could be faster than me.

All three librarians have guns, and they point them right at me. Two red laser dots

I loved it when the HEAD library Ninja said 'Shhhhh! This isn't a nightclub,' AND then karate-chopped all their HEADs off!

rest on my chest. I feel one on my forehead. This is worse than anything I'd imagined.

The librarians move slowly up the steps towards me, weapons raised. As they close in I realise that their 'guns' are actually barcode scanners, the kind they use at the front desk of the library, so I turn and run, praying that Sweat Pants doesn't catch me. As I do, a large male librarian emerges from the double front doors. He has a forehead so greasy it almost blinds me with reflected sunlight. He's brandishing a large net, like a dog catcher.

'Take it easy, buddy.' He goes to nab me and I run the other way. Two more librarians rappel on ropes from the roof. They are dressed in black cardigans and black pants like Library Ninjas. They land on the ground in front of me, unclip their harnesses and

Library Ninja

train their barcode scanner beams on my legs.

'No place to run, kid,' says Sweat Pants, who is now close enough that I can read her name badge: Sienna Harper-Hill – Head of Youth Services. A librarian with the initials 'SHH'.

I am surrounded by a narrowing circle of librarians on the front steps. The alarm beeps loudly, the red light flashes, illuminating

my face in sickening swirls of light. There's
a crowd building now. Two perfect-looking
parents holding library books across the street
cover their perfect-looking children's eyes.
People inside the library are lined up at the
windows, watching.

And I'm standing here, naked. (Not *actually*
naked. It's a metaphor for how I feel on the
inside.)

'You thought you'd get away with it, didn't
you?' It's the Head of Youth Services – *SHH*.
She's actually kind of cute. Beautiful in a
Sasha-ish way. This makes me even more
nervous. My bladder, all of a sudden, feels full.

'N-no,' I say.

'You did, didn't you?'

'No, ma'am.' I'm not sure why I call her
'ma'am'. She's only about 25.

'You think we're running a charity here? You think we like chasing horrible little kids to get our property back? You think books grow on trees?'

'No. Well, technically, they do but –'

'Don't get smart with me. How do you think we feel when our books come back half-eaten by a pet cockatoo?'

'I don't know. I don't have a pet c–'

'Or soaked in cat wee?'

'Um . . . not good?' I say. A little bit of vomit burns the back of my throat. Cat wee has never been one of my favourite smells.

'Or with a used Band-Aid for a bookmark?'

I shake my head. 'That's right. Not good.'

She's in real close now, and I'd like to say that her breath smells like two dead dogs and that she has sleep nuggets in her eyes and loads of orange earwax . . . but none of those things is true. And she smells good, like daffodils. (I'm not totally sure what they smell like, but I have a hunch that this is it.) I try not to fall in love with her, but it's very difficult.

'So, what do I do with you?' she asks.

'Maybe . . . let me go?'

She laughs out loud and rests a hand on my back, which feels kind of nice. 'I'm afraid library policy in a situation such as this is to give you "the treatment".'

'What's the –'
I begin.

LIBROCIRCUMPHOBIA :

The fear of Being surrounded BY a group OF Librarians.

The other librarians gather closer, tightening the circle, grinning like maniacs.

'You survive the treatment, I wipe your fine,' she says.

She pulls morning tea out of her backpack. There are lamingtons, a sponge cake and individual lemon meringue pies.

This is the punishment? They're going to make me eat pie? Bring it on. I love pie.

All seven librarians choose a lamington, a slice of cake or a pie. I reach out for a treat and the Head of Youth Services slaps my hand. 'Not for naughty boys,' she says.

They stand there and eat the morning tea right in front of me. It's torture. They are the plumpest, most delicious-looking lamingtons I have ever seen – a light, fluffy cake, thick with chocolate, and cream in the middle.

The librarians have cream all over their lips and they guzzle cups of tea from a tall floral thermos, poured by the greasy guy with the dog catcher's net. My stomach lets out a deep, Jurassic groan. When the last bite of morning tea is gone, Sienna Harper-Hill licks the Tupperware container, giving herself a coconut moustache.

Next, she pulls a book from her KBPL library bag. The others reach in and take out a book, too. They open them up, each gripping a single, razor-sharp page, and they swipe and slash the paper at me. I try to move out of the way but one of them cuts the sleeve off my T-shirt.

'Ow!'

Another one slices my shirt right across the chest.

'Hey!'

They deliver paper cuts with such terrible accuracy that within a minute my shirt is in shreds.

'Alright, that's enough!' Sienna Harper-Hill jerks her head and two of the others grab me by the arms and escort me inside.

NEver let a librarian:
(3 Golden rules)

1. Corner you with a barcodE scaNNer.
2. Catch you looking at DOG videos on the library computer (they're strictly cAt people).
3. Tell you tHe time of day. They will ALWAYs lie. (they want you in the library FOREVER!)

'Where are you taking me?'

'One last challenge,' Harper-Hill grunts. The others titter and snort.

Never let a librarian take you to a second location. I'm sure I've heard this sometime.

Library customers watch me from behind their books and computer screens as I am led past 'Magazines and Non-Fiction'. My captors take me behind the front counter and park me at a section marked 'Information'. There is a long queue of people with angry, twisted faces.

'You're to deal with public complaints until the library closes.'

'But I–'

'About time,' says an elderly lady with a scrinched-up face who can barely see over the counter. I don't think I've ever seen anything as old as her. Not even in a museum.

'I want to know where I can plug in my blender,' she says.

'I'm sorry?' I say.

'Don't be sorry. Just show me where an outlet is.'

She actually has a milkshake-maker under her arm and two litres of Lite White in her hand. I turn for backup but the librarians are all busy doing their own thing.

'Um, I'm pretty sure you can't make milkshakes in the library,' I say.

'Is this the library?' she asks.

And it gets worse. Over the next two and a half hours, I am treated to a parade of the strangest humans and weirdest questions I have ever heard. They include:

'Could you please rip off this Band-Aid for me?'

'What time do you stop serving breakfast?'

'It's so hot outside. Is the sun getting bigger?'

'How many books on maths problems would you have left if I checked out eight?'

'Did a lady with a tattoo of a gecko on her neck just come in here?'

'Could you help me find some examples of Ancient Greek AFL players?'

'Can you mind my cat for a couple of hours?'

And . . .

'Do you have a recent photo of Captain Cook?'

It takes half an hour to boot everyone out of the library at the end of the day. Sienna Harper-Hill leads me over to the front counter. She types, rapid-fire, into the computer. She still has coconut on her face.

Ten seconds later, a brand-new library card slides out of the card printer. She picks it up and presents me with it. 'What do you say?'

'Thank you.' Although I'm not sure I ever want to come into the library again.

'Good luck getting your act together,' she says. 'Would you like to borrow anything before you go?'

'Um . . .' I think for a minute. I'm still reeling from the three-pronged torture. My shirt and mind are in shreds. But there *is* one book I'm really curious about.

'Could I possibly re-borrow *Fungus the Bogeyman?*' I ask.

She tilts her head to the side, not understanding.

'I didn't actually get around to reading it.'

What Would You Rather Do?

Jack and I had a 15-hour bus ride to Canberra last week for a school excursion. Apart from the roadkill-spotting competition and Sophie Smith vomiting bright-green soft drink on the driver's back, the highlight of the trip was an epic game of 'What Would You Rather Do?'. Here are some of our best:

Would you rather . . .?

* Have your kidney removed without anaesthetic or declare your love for your teacher in front of the entire school?

* Have pimples all over your face from age 12 to 18 or have pimples all over your bottom for the rest of your life?

* Eat an entire boiled pumpkin or two kilos of raw potatoes?

* Be five years old or 50 years old for the next year?

* Eat an entire aeroplane or eat 18 bicycles and seven televisions? (Frenchman Michel Lotito ate all of these things in his lifetime. He was known as 'Monsieur Mangetout' or 'Mr Eats All'. NB: Planes, bicycles and televisions are all gluten-free, but planes are sometimes produced in factories containing sesame seeds.)

I would SURE love to eat that AEROPLANE.

MONSIEUR MANGETOUT

* Lick a pig's trotter or an elephant's bottom?

* Take on Captain Jack Sparrow in a sword fight or Darth Vader in a lightsaber duel?

* Secretly eat camel poo or have everyone at school think you ate camel poo when you actually didn't?

* Become rich and famous for something really embarrassing or remain poor and unknown for the rest of your life?

* Win a lifetime's supply of doughnuts but have to share each one with your worst enemy or never eat another doughnut again?

* Get bitten by a shark while out surfing or be swallowed whole by a whale and spat out onto the rocks?

* See your best friend go to jail for a year for a crime that you committed or go to jail yourself for five years?

* Kick your foot on a rock and rip off your big toenail or have your tongue pierced with a nail?

* Eat an extra-large barbecued seagull with chips or a small baked hamster with mash?

If you can think of any good ones, email them to me at thetomweekly@gmail.com and maybe I'll put them in my next book and include your name.

Barbecued
SEAGULL
with chips
(well-done!)

WHEN SOCKS COME BACK

'Honestly, I don't know where they go, Tom Weekly.'

Mum is sitting next to me on the couch, folding a mountain of clothes. It's Mother's Day tomorrow, and I'm secretly hoping she gets through all the washing before the morning so that I won't have to do it.

'Seven socks and not a single matching pair,' she goes on. 'Where do you put them?'

'Uggh,' I grunt, praying that she won't

continue to bother me while my favourite show, *World's Deadliest Cats*, is on.

'Don't "Uggh" me – I'm serious. You wear them, and then where do they go? And only one. You never lose the whole pair!'

'Mum. It's a pair of socks! I'm watching a show.'

Sig, my favourite character, has two minutes to bathe Tigger – one of the most vicious Persians in America. If she can't do it, she goes into elimination and could be voted out of the Cattery.

I'M outta here!

'Don't "It's a pair of socks" me. If you spent less time watching TV and more time looking after your belongings, we wouldn't have this problem.'

I mute the TV and look at her. 'I don't think you understand how important this show is to me.'

'I don't think you understand how important these socks are to me. They cost a small fortune.'

I shake my head and study my mother for a moment, her face all scrunched up. I make a mental note to never become an adult, not if it means caring this much about socks. She only ever buys the cheap polyester ones anyway. They make my feet sweat like a dog in a sauna, and I'm developing a greenish fungus between my toes. I long for an all-natural fibre. Now that would be something to make a fuss about.

'You can start buying them out of your pocket money, Thomas. If you pay for them yourself, you might value them,' she snips.

'No way!'

'Yes way. I'll be putting this week's pocket money towards socks.'

'That's not fair!'

Fabled Sock Hunter
Sir Edwin Hoofwear

'Well then, you'd better find some socks.'

I growl at her, switch off the TV and head for the laundry.

My pocket money was due to be paid this afternoon. She doesn't realise it but that money was going to buy her Mother's Day present – an ugly crystal horse that she likes in the gift shop on Jonson Street.

Bando, my Labrador retriever, follows me into the laundry. At least he likes me. I snap on the light, flip open the lid of the dirty clothes hamper and start digging for socks. Moments later, I'm pretty sure I've struck gold. I pull my hand out and am clutching a pair of what can only be my sister Tanya's frilly knickers. I squeal and fling them across the room. They slip down the wall behind the washing machine. I lunge at the sink, flip on the tap and scrub my hand with Dynamo.

I wish I could scrub my mind of what I've just seen.

Bando bumps against my leg, then turns and snarls at the clothes dryer. He does that sometimes. I don't think he likes the noise it makes.

I dry my hands and get down on my knees to look inside the dryer, hoping to find a missing sock that might win back my pocket money. It's pretty dark in there. I reach in. It's empty and deep.

Bando growls again.

'It's okay, boy. I'm not going to turn it on. Hellooo!' I call into the black pit.

'Who are you saying "hello" to?' Mum yells from the lounge room.

'No one!'

Bando barks at the dryer. My eyes start to adjust to the darkness but I still can't see how far back it stretches. It's no wonder socks go missing.

I pull my head out of the dryer and grab the torch from the toolbox in the linen closet. I kneel back down and flick the torch on, but the batteries are dead. I stretch my arm in to feel for socks, but I can't reach the back wall of the dryer. I squeeze my head and shoulders inside the small, round opening. I balance my stomach on the rim of the door, but I still can't reach the back. I make a final lunge and tip forward, overbalancing. I reach out to stop myself, but all I feel is empty space and blind panic.

'Muuuum!'

I tumble into darkness, free-falling and somersaulting once, twice, then *whump!*

IN the dryer, no oNe can hear you <u>SCREAM</u>

The impact punches the wind out of me. I'm on my back, looking up, and the white circle of light where I entered the dryer looks like the moon in a night sky. Down here it's pitch black.

I dig my fingers into the soft surface beneath me. Something stinks like the potato storage room under Brent Bunder's chip shop.

I sit up, still clutching the torch, and flick the switch back and forth – nothing happens. I know this must be a dream but I don't care. I want out. I open my eyes as wide as I can, trying to will myself out of the dream.

'Mum!' I scream, my voice sounding pathetic and small. 'Ma!'

Bando barks, but it sounds so far away.

I smack the torch hard against the palm of my hand. The light flickers for a moment and then dies. I do it again and the weak beam stays lit. I whip the light around in scared, jerky movements. Specks of lint float past my face. I'm in what appears to be a small dungeon, maybe three metres by three metres. It's warm and the air is dry and scratchy in my throat. The walls, floor and ceiling are peppered with bright spots of colour. As my eyes adjust and I look more closely, I realise what these bright spots are.

Socks.

Hundreds, maybe thousands, of socks.

I have never seen so many socks in one place.

I even see a sock that I recognise – a Ninja Turtle sock hanging from the wall, from a time when I was obsessed with Donatello. I train my torch beam on it and reach out to pick it off the wall. Then I recognise the sock next to it, too – a yellow skate sock with a blood stain on the ankle. The sock next to that is mine as well. In fact, they are all mine: baby socks, soccer socks, school socks, bed socks. One lone sock from every pair I've ever owned.

I laugh out loud. I have fallen directly into the answer to my problem. I'll stuff my pockets and shirt with these socks. I'll bust out of here and, when I hand them to Mum, she'll have no choice but to give back my pocket money, plus a bonus. *Boom*.

I grab the Ninja Turtle sock and feel a hot, sharp pain in my thumb. I train the torch onto my hand and see a red bite mark there, like a small child has bitten me.

I go to grab the yellow skate sock and feel that same white-hot pain tear through my hand. I reel back and discover two bites. This is insane. Socks can't bite. I switch the torch to the other hand and reach down to grab a bunch of socks from the floor, but I am bitten hard, over and over again.

'OW!' I scream, and Bando barks again from high above.

I rub the bites, trying to make the pain go away. I focus the weak torch glow on the floor and see the strangest thing – the socks appear to be moving. Not much, just a gentle wriggle, like furry little snakes. I think I might have woken them. I lean down close and watch. They wriggle and squirm and slide over one another. The mouths of the socks open and close like hungry goldfish. They look quite cute, until I see the rows of fine, jagged teeth.

I swear I can hear them now, too, squeaking like little chipmunks. This is the weirdest dream I have ever had. I need to grab some socks and get out of here.

I reach down verrrry slowly and gather a handful of socks. They twitch and twist in my grip. They bite my fingers, but I don't care. I stuff a fistful of the squirming zombie socks down the neck of my shirt. They attach themselves to my chest and belly like leeches, biting me hard.

I accidentally drop the torch and it's instantly swallowed by the socks. I reach around but it's gone. The socks' squeaking

chatter grows louder, and they start to worm
their way up my legs.

'HELP!' I scream into the darkness, and
the only answer is Bando's barking.

They slither up my body and over my
neck and face. I try to call out again but
a sock covers my mouth, muffling my cry.
I am so stupid – if I had taken better care of

my socks I wouldn't be here. Now my mother will wake up tomorrow with no Mother's Day present. And no son.

I look up at the dryer opening and see Bando's head poking through the hole. He has something in his jaws – it looks like his extendable lead – and he's shaking his head from side to side. The lead is uncoiling down towards me.

The socks continue to attack, covering my entire body now, and I am in so much pain. I try to rip them off but new socks seem to replace them. I wonder how many other kids have died this way? Death by sock.

I reach out and grab the lead's plastic handle. I feel tension in the cord, pulling me up, and Bando's head is no longer visible. My feet rise off the floor and I clutch the handle tightly with both hands. Bando is rescuing me. This is amazing. He's usually so selfish and lazy. I've heard of dogs rescuing their owners from snow storms, but never from sock pits.

As I rise through the darkness towards the light I am filled with hope that I might make it out of this alive. My head is hot, my skin is itchy and sore all over, and the smell of socks makes me feel like throwing up. But I am slowly, surely, rising from my sockish dungeon.

Then I look down and see something truly horrifying – the socks seem to be linking up. They are joining forces to form one long, anaconda-like monster. The snake sways and stretches up towards my foot, snapping at me as I approach the dryer opening.

Almost at the top, I pray that the lead won't snap before I get there. I reach out towards the metal rim of the dryer with one hand and just grasp it with the tips of my fingers. I pull myself up with every ounce of strength I have, feeling the anasockda winding itself around my left foot. I hook one arm over the rim and I am born again as my head emerges into the light.

The sock snake tries to pull me down but I kick hard one final time and pull myself through the hole, falling onto the tiled laundry floor. There is a moist feeling in my ear and a loud slurping sound as Bando licks me. He barks ferociously at the dryer and snaps at the anasockda as it slowly recoils back into the depths.

I tear the socks away from my face and neck. I spit out the sock in my mouth and cough up

a large, slimy lint ball into the palm of my
hand. I flick it into the sink and rip the last
remaining socks off my body and my legs.
I lie on the tiled floor, sucking in one
enormous breath after another.

'Mum?' I call.

It's quiet for a moment, then I hear
footsteps before Mum comes into the room.
'What on earth are you doing now? What's
happened to you?'

I am sweating and panting, but I am alive.

'You look like you've been bitten. What
happened?'

'Zombie socks,' I say, enjoying the coolness
of the tiles on my skin.

'You're a strange child, Tom. Let me have
a look at you. And where did you get all those
socks?'

There are about 30 socks on the floor – fluffy, hairy, sad little things. But they are lifeless now. All the fight's gone out of them. They no longer squeak or squirm.

I push myself up. Bando continues to bark into the mouth of the dryer. I poke the socks on the floor with my toe but they don't react.

'Where did they come from?' Mum asks.

'Back from the dead.' I'm not sure if I'm talking about the socks or me.

'I hope you're not coming down with something. Go and have a lie down.'

'Can I have my pocket money now?' I ask.

'Well . . .' She picks up the pile of socks and tries to think of a reason why not.

'Thanks,' I say before she has a chance to respond.

I give the socks one last look. They lie limply in her arms. I must be going mad. I head out of the laundry and down the hall. Peace and pocket money have been restored. Mum will receive the ugly crystal horse in the morning and I will, once again, be her favourite child.

I stumble into my room, skin still stinging all over. I flop down on the bed, wishing that I was just a normal, dumb kid without an imagination who didn't have things like this happen to him all the time. *Zombie socks,* I think. *Mum is right. I am a strange child.*

I hear a scream.

'Tom!' It's the voice Mum uses when she sees a spider and needs me to catch it. 'TOM!'

I jump off my bed and run into the hall to see the most hideous thing I have ever seen – my mother's body riddled with zombie socks.

'TOOOOMMMMM!' she howls.

Continued from page 64

Revenge of the Nits
(Part Two):
Lice-ensed to Kill

I fall headfirst from the window ledge onto the concrete path beside Lewis's house. The dog-sized nit falls from the window behind me. It slams down on my chest and stretches its bloodsucking feeding tubes towards my scalp. Its eyes swirl, hungering for human blood.

I look up the path to check that Lewis isn't watching, then I punch the giant insect hard in the nose and throw him to the ground.

I grab the camera, get a quick shot of the louse doing a backspin on the path, then scramble to my feet and bolt towards the front of the house. Lewis and Jack have stopped dead in the front yard. Jack squeals like he has seen something truly terrifying.

He has.

A plague of hungry, salivating lice swarms from the front door of the shabby weatherboard house and into the overgrown yard. I film it all. The long grass is alive with scurrying knee-high nits; it's like they're running through a lush green head of hair. When they see us, or smell our blood, they charge.

'RUUUUUN!' Jack screams.

Lewis and I are right on his heels.

'Fire station!' Lewis shouts. 'On the corner.'

I can see the fire station two blocks away, next to the police station. About 300 metres from here. If you want to improve your short-distance running times, I highly recommend inviting a horde of killer head lice to your next sports carnival.

We slow at Tennyson Street for cars to go by and Jack calls, 'Cop!' He points straight ahead and, sure enough, driving towards us on the other side of the street is a police car.

'HEY!' I shout, flinging my arms in the air to wave the car down. 'STOP!'

When the traffic clears, we dash

PEEKABOO!

across the street, the nits almost upon us. The police car pulls up at the Give Way sign. The officer at the wheel is eating a sandwich. He drops it and his mouth forms a capital 'O' when he sees the mutant nit army bearing down on him. I rip open the back door and the three of us pile in. Jack slams it shut.

'What's going on?' the officer demands. His mayonnaise-spattered moustache wiggles when he speaks. I recognise him right away – Sergeant John Hategarden, the officer who arrested Mr Skroop for chopping up my football and eating the prize scab from my collection.

'Nits!' I tell him, breathing hard from the run. 'They've mutated.'

'I just saw one eat a cat,' Jack says.

'As if!' I say, just as a nit the size of a small horse appears at the window. It fogs the glass with its breath. It has a furry grey-and-white tail hanging from its mouth.

'I think that's Cookie, the cat from next door,' Lewis says.

Cookie's tail looks bristly and lashes from side to side like my cat Gordon's when he's ready to pounce. The nit makes a loud sucking noise and the cat's tail disappears like a string of spaghetti.

'Poor Cookie,' Lewis says.

'Anyone know how to perform the Heimlich manoeuvre on a nit?' I ask.

Then the nit convulses, its mouth jerks open, and it coughs the cat back up, like a giant furball, onto the road. Cookie screams across the street and up a palm tree, clinging to the trunk with its claws, shaking nit spit off its coat.

We cheer and the monstrous nit slams its hairy claw against the glass. Another freakishly large louse leaps onto the front of the car, denting the bonnet. The insect stares in at us with its cold, grey eyes. It pulls back its alien head and smashes it against the windscreen, sending a spider web of cracks shooting out from the centre of the glass. Jack, Lewis and I scream and hug one another in the back seat.

Hategarden panics and boots the accelerator, gunning the car across the intersection, right through the head lice swarm. The nits, quick on their feet, scatter to the side of the road. We speed back up the street. The mutant nit on the bonnet has its extraterrestrial face pressed hard against the glass. It grips the wipers in its pincers and glares at me in a way that says, *You will pay dearly for this, my little friend.*

Hategarden slams the brakes at about 70 kilometres an hour, sending the mini-beast flying backwards off the front window and onto the road. It rips off the windscreen wipers, hits the tar hard, bounces, skids and bowls the nit army over like tenpins.

Jack cheers and claps. '*That* was awesome.'

Lewis punches him in the arm. 'I think he just knocked over Todd and Millie – my two favourite nits.'

Jack and I look at one another, suddenly more scared of Lewis than we are of the head lice.

'Do you think they're okay?' Lewis asks.

'Whaddya mean?' Jack fires back. 'He would've sucked out our brains.'

'Nits don't eat brains,' Lewis says.

The other lice scurry to the injured nits' rescue. They assess the damage . . . then they eat Todd and Millie right there on the road in front of us.

'But it looks like they eat each other,' Jack says.

Lewis covers his eyes. I capture it all on camera. This will either win me the 'Most Disgusting Documentary Film' award at the

Oscars, or it will get our movie banned in several countries. Maybe both.

Hategarden starts to drive off but the lice get vicious now. They swarm the car, attacking with their razor-sharp claws. Hategarden revs the engine but the car can't move under the weight of the lice. There are so many nits on top of us that it's almost dark in here.

'I don't wanna diiiie!' Jack cries.

'We're not gonna die!' I yell at him over the noise of the nits jumping on the roof and beating at the windows. There is a loud *POP!* as the rear tyres explode, then the front ones go. I can smell fuel, too.

'Okay, maybe we are going to die,' I tell him, 'but not without a fight.'

'Mayday, mayday!' Hategarden barks into his walkie-talkie. 'Sergeant John Hategarden and three children trapped in a police vehicle on Keats Street. Immediate assistance required. Repeat, immediate –' His words are swallowed by the smashing and pounding of lice trying to rip the vehicle open like a tin of beans.

'They leave me no choice,' Hategarden shouts. He pulls his firearm from its holster.

'NO!' Lewis tells him. 'They're my pets!'

'I'm sorry, son,' Hategarden says. 'I'm an animal lover, too, but these aren't animals. They're monsters. Block your ears!'

We do, and Hategarden fires three shots into the roof of the car – *BANG! BANG! BANG!*

Red and green lice blood oozes through the holes. The lice leap away, daylight returns, and the terrible scratching sound of nit claws on metal falls silent. They leave a three- or four-metre ring around the car, watching us like a gaggle of angry, nervous lobsters circling a boiling pot of water.

'GO!' Jack pleads.

But within seconds the nits close in on us again, slamming us from both sides, buckling the car doors with their rock-hard heads. This is what life on Lewis's scalp must be like – savage and treacherous.

Hategarden fires three more shots into the roof and the lice flee again. He revs the engine hard.

'Ha! See ya, suckers!' Jack shouts. Then the motor chokes and dies. *What happened?*

Hategarden tries to start the car again. I am very aware of the sharp stench of petrol.

'It won't . . .' Hategarden spits. 'They've drained the tank.' He slams his foot up and down on the accelerator, turns the wheel left and right, and twists the key – but the car will not start. He bangs the wheel as though that might make the car move.

'How many more bullets do you have?' Jack asks.

Hategarden glances over his shoulder at us with a look that says, *None*. I take the camera away from my eye, realising what this means.

The circling nits look ready to attack again.

'I want my mummyyyy,' Jack says.

'QUIET!' Hategarden screams.

'Let me speak to them,' Lewis says, nervously kneading his hands together. 'I can do this.'

'Lewis.'

'Trust me,' he says. 'I know what I'm doing.'

I look out at the slavering jaws on the circle of six-legged assassins.

'I'm not sure they want to talk,' I say.

Lewis starts to rock back and forth gently in his seat.

'Are you okay?' I ask.

He breathes deeply, in a husky whine. Jack and I look at each other, worried.

'Lewis?' I say.

He makes the loudest, scratchiest, screechiest noise I have ever heard. A sound that could cut glass. I block my ears and beg him to stop, but he won't.

'What are you doing, kid?' Hategarden demands, blocking his ears too, but Lewis keeps rocking and screeching, his eyes wide open, trance-like. I'm waiting for his head to start spinning.

'I think he's scared,' I tell Hategarden. 'He's losing it.'

In the background, one of the lice starts to make the same noise that Lewis is making, but maybe higher pitched, like a cicada. Seconds later another nit starts up, and another, until there is a chirruping nit chorus all around us.

Lewis reaches across me and opens the door.

'Don't,' I tell him, but he won't listen.

The door scrapes, metal on metal, as he shoves it open.

'STOP!' I yell, grabbing him by the arm, but he tears himself free and walks away from the car, towards the festival of lice.

'I never liked him much anyway,' Jack says.

I whack him on the arm.

Hategarden tries to open his door, but it's buckled so badly it won't budge. 'Hey!' he shouts. 'Get back in here. You got a death wish, kid?'

Lewis walks slowly, fearlessly, towards his pets – screeching in unison with them. As he reaches the circle, he comes face to face with insects big and ferocious enough to eat him in two bites. Three of the bugs stare him right in the eyes, and others from around the circle start to gather closer.

I cover my face, peeking out from between my fingers, preparing for the worst. But, rather than devouring Lewis right there and then, the wall of lice opens. It's like a door to a secret passageway, and only Lewis holds the key. As he passes through, his nits begin to follow him. Lewis strides across the lawn towards his house, followed by his swarm of oversized friends. He is the Pied Piper of the nit world.

We all watch in awe as he stops at the tap, picks up the hose and turns it on. He scrubs the sauce out of his hair, then shakes like a dog after a bath. He continues to communicate in Louse as hundreds of nits line up and he hoses them clean of Nan's secret sauce one at a time. The nits shrink before our eyes, just like they did in the bath.

Before they get too small to see, Lewis leans down and the nits climb into his hair, disappearing into the foliage. He repeats this until the street is clear of lice and the near-deafening screech of the nit symphony is replaced by the sound of approaching sirens.

LEWIS

Nit wHisperer

Epilogue

The following day, Sergeant Hategarden and another police officer have a few questions for Nan about the ingredients in her sauce. I have a few myself. Questions like, 'What the heck was in it?' and 'Are you out of your mind?' and 'Could you try to make a sauce that works on humans because it would be really cool to be a giant for a day?'

I am there in her living room when the police interview her. She serves them Anzac biscuits and a cup of tea, but I notice that they don't eat or drink.

'So, what exactly was in the sauce, Mrs Weekly?' Hategarden asks.

'Oh, I don't know, love – a few things.'

'What kinds of things?'

'Well, tomatoes, vinegar, spices.'

'Right,' he says, jotting notes in his little black notebook. 'Is that all?'

'A little bit of bleach.'

'Bleach? But bleach could kill you!'

'To keep the bugs out. My mother always put a dash of bleach in her cup of tea and a dash in her spaghetti sauce. Keeps your dishes clean and your insides spick 'n' span. And a tablespoon of bicarb soda to keep your teeth nice and white. There was a little bit of pine-lime shaving cream for flavour, a clove of garlic and a pinch of VapoRub for the sinuses and . . .'

Hategarden writes down everything in Nan's secret spaghetti sauce recipe. There are 136 ingredients in all. Most of them are more likely to be found in the chemist or the hardware store than the supermarket.

Hategarden sends the recipe on to the CSIRO, the national science agency. They grow two cockroaches the size of meerkats and several mice the size of Chihuahuas. But that's off the record. For some reason, Nan's toxic spaghetti sauce does not work on humans.

Lewis, Jack and I get an 'F' on our filmmaking assignment. Miss Norrish thinks we've used a special effects package to create the 'unnecessarily gory and entirely unbelievable' action sequence, which was against the rules of the assignment. I try to tell her that it all happened, just as I filmed it,

REVENGE OF tHE KILLER NITS! (PG)

and she threatens to send me to the principal for telling lies.

But we do get pinned with medals of bravery by the Kings Bay Police Department in a private ceremony. I suggest that, since Jack screamed, 'I don't wanna diiiie!' and 'I want my mummyyyy!', he might not qualify for a bravery medal, but Hategarden gives him one anyway.

Oh, and Lewis still has nits.

25 Reasons Why I Can't Wait to Be in a Nursing Home

My pop, Cliff Weekly, used to try to escape from Kings Bay Nursing Home every second week. I never understood why. He was living my dream life. Here are 25 reasons why I can't wait to be in a nursing home:

1. Room service 24/7, and I won't have to waste energy trimming my toenails and nose-hairs and wiping my bottom. Someone will do it for me!

2. No homework.
   (My teachers will have died years ago.)

3. Nude bingo.

4. Wheelchair races in the hallway.

5. Wheelchair jousting in the tearoom.

6. Wheelchair scuba diving in the pool.

7. Dinner tray sled races down the grassy hill near the bin shed.

8. Borrowing a fellow inmate's motor scooter and laying some doughnuts in the car park out front.

9. Bed sores make awesome scabs, and scab collecting is one of my favourite pastimes.

10. Catch 'n' kiss. Old ladies can't run as fast as the girls in my class.

11. Dinner at 3 pm.

12. Nap time at 9 am, 11:15 am, 1:05 pm, 3:22 pm, 4:05 pm and lights out by 5 pm.

13. Replacing the oxygen tanks with helium so that everyone speaks in high-pitched voices.

14. Nice soft food so the food fights won't hurt as much.

15. Not having to brush my teeth. (No teeth to brush.)

I love a GOOD Lamb roAst!

16. Wearing those cool old-guy nappies so I won't have to walk all the way to the toilet during the ad breaks.

17. Speaking about myself in the third person. As in, 'You wouldn't mind trimming that festering wart off Poppa's knee, would you?'

18. Tricking my grandkids into smuggling Chupa Chups in for me.

19. Pinching their cheeks really hard when they come to visit.

20. Eating really slowly to annoy the nurses.

21. Eating custard and jelly in little plastic containers after every meal.

22. Annoying people with stupid requests like, 'Be a dear and peel those grapes for me, would you, love?'

23. Spending all my superannuation money on corn chips and ginger beer at the vending machine down the hall.

24. If there's an awesome room with a great view that I really want, I probably won't have to wait too long for it to become available.

25. Unlimited time on my hands.
(Ish. I'll be 97.)

Pop's most spectacular nursing home breakout attempt is documented in 'The Great Escape' in *My Life & Other Massive Mistakes*.

NB: Some of my friends helped brainstorm this list. Their names are in the back of this book.

The Clappers

Jack and I have started a band. It's not like
any other band you've ever heard. It's edgy,
it's experimental, it's ahead of its time. See,
we can't really play any instruments. And we
can't sing. But we can clap.

You might think that an all-clapping
band sounds kind of terrible, but you would
be wrong. We're *awesemic*. We've always
been good at clapping, ever since we were
little. When we were about six, Jack would
start clapping a simple beat, then I'd join in,

and pretty soon we'd have a song. Until now, we've kept this extraordinary talent to ourselves. It was just something we did. But something this good can't stay a secret forever.

Our chance comes just before lunch today when Mrs McDonald makes an announcement over the crackly PA system at school: 'Due to an unfortunate outbreak of hypochondria, the Year Three riverdance troupe is unable to perform at tonight's Christmas Concert. Anyone who would like to stage a skit or musical number should report to Mr Skroop's office at the beginning of lunch. Thank you.'

Jack and I are sitting at the back of the classroom. I look at him. 'Did you know that if you perform in the show you get the day off tomorrow?'

Jack grins. Tomorrow is the last day of school for the year, and we'd do pretty much anything to skip it and get a head start on summer holidays.

'Shame we don't have any talent,' Jack says.

The bell rings.

'You may *quietly* pack up your things and go to lunch,' Miss Norrish says.

'What do you mean we don't have talent?'

We start packing up our stuff.

'I mean, we can't –'

'The Clappers!' I tell him.

Jack looks at me blankly. Kids spill out of the classroom while Miss Norrish cleans the whiteboard.

'We are *not* doing The Clappers in public,' he whispers firmly.

'Yes, we are.' I grab him by the arm and try to drag him out the door, but he won't budge. 'You *love* doing The Clappers.'

'Not in front of actual people,' he says.

'It's time we unleash our insane skills on the world,' I tell him.

'People will laugh at us.'

'Laughers gonna laugh,' I say.

'What does that even mean?'

'It means who cares what they say!'

'You actually believe that?'

'No, but do you want the day off school or not?' I ask.

'Outside please, boys,' Miss Norrish says, grabbing a stack of books from her desk and heading for the classroom door.

Jack looks at me.

I look at him.

Jack growls.

We head for Skroop's office.

The deputy principal's door is big and dark, and we are almost alone in the dimly lit hallway. There is just one other contender for the last available Christmas Concert slot: Scarlet Grady, a Year Two girl who eats grass in the bottom playground every lunchtime. She has a creepy ventriloquist's dummy on her lap, and she's making the dummy speak in an annoying high-pitched voice: 'Season's greetings, my pretties.' It makes me shiver, but she's actually pretty good at not moving her mouth.

'You ready?' I ask.

'No,' Jack replies.

I clench my fist and knock quietly on Skroop's door. We wait. The red carpet beneath our feet is like a river of blood flowing down the hall. Maybe from all the other kids who dared disturb Walton Skroop from his lair.

THERE is something about Mr Skroop that unnerves ME.

'This is a bad idea,' Jack says.

The door *screeeeks* open and a dark, cloaked figure appears. His face is half in shadow. His eyes glow red. He laughs a hideous, twisted laugh, like a train crash.

That's what I hear and see anyway.

What actually happens is that Skroop appears eating an Iced VoVo biscuit and holding a World's Best Teacher mug (which I'm pretty sure he bought for himself). He is wearing his maroon jumper, shredded at the shoulder from the claws of his evil cat, Mr Fatterkins.

'You two . . .' he says, disgusted.

We stare up into his large nostrils. They are like black holes that could swallow us if he were to sniff.

'What do you want?'

'Well, w-w-we we –' I begin.

'Wee wee wee,' Skroop mocks. 'If you need to do a wee-wee, I suggest you use the latrines. Now spit it out, boy.'

I swallow hard, finding it difficult to breathe.

'We w-would like to perform at the Christmas Concert,' I stammer.

'Really,' he says, lowering his voice. 'And what would you two insignificant, flat-footed, jelly-back-boned, knock-kneed little prawns like to perform?'

This really makes me nervous. The last time Mr Skroop called me that name was when we accidentally burnt down his fence with a tiki torch, nearly set fire to his cat and had him arrested by Sergeant Hategarden.

'The C-Clappers,' I say.

I can feel Jack shrivelling next to me.

'What is The C-Clappers?' Skroop asks.

'Well, you see, Jack and I have a band and —'

Jack treads on my toe, begging me to stop, but I won't. This is The Clappers' chance to

go public and nothing – not even Skroop –
will get in our way.

'We clap,' I finish. 'We clap songs.'

Skroop smiles, baring those brown, gappy
teeth and wheezing stale coffee breath right in
our faces. 'Wonderful!' he says.

I smile, relieved. 'Really?'

Even Jack smiles.

'No. Not really,' Skroop snaps. 'You'll make
fools of yourselves but, as there appear to be
no other takers for the slot . . .'

His eyes darken and he smacks Scarlet Grady
with a glare of pure evil. Her dummy squeaks,
'Help!' and she scurries off down the hall.

'I shall see you tonight,' Skroop finishes
with a smile. 'I can hardly wait.'

He slams the door in our faces.

Jack and I stand there in the darkened

hallway for a moment, silent, the river of
blood lapping around our ankles.

'We're in!' I say, grinning.

It's 3:34 pm, and Jack and I are in my garage
for our first and only rehearsal before
tonight's concert. We're squeezed between
Mum's car and the wall, which is pretty
uncomfortable. Jack sits on a bag of stinky
garden manure, and I'm sitting on the mower.
Mum has asked us to be quiet three times
so far. She's trying to watch a recording of
Australia's Got Talent, her favourite show. She
says we sound terrible.

'We've got to expect people not to "get" us,'
I tell Jack. 'All geniuses are misunderstood. Did
you know that Colonel Sanders' chicken recipe

was rejected over a thousand times before someone agreed to buy it and KFC was born?'

'There was a reason it took so long,' Jack says. 'Have you ever tasted it?'

I shake my head. 'I don't even know you anymore.'

Ever since he fell in love with Aurora, the new girl who's a vegan, he's been making snide remarks about meat and junk food.

'Let's take it from the top. Okay . . . one, two . . . one, two, three . . .' and I start in on 'We Wish You a Merry Christmas', but it's out of time and Jack just sits there, glaring at me.

I stop.

'The show's in three hours. If we don't rehearse, we'll –'

'Have you ever *heard* of a clapping band?' Jack asks, poking his finger into the bag of

A rare photo of the
MYTHICAL Brownee 'the hands'
Magee clapping his last
performance in 1953.

garden manure he's sitting on. He pulls out a chunk, sniffs it, then almost chokes on his own tongue before dropping the manure to the floor.

'What did you expect?' I ask.

He ignores me. 'Do you know *why* you haven't heard of a clapping band?'

'Because we're bold, radical dudes and this is a world-first?'

'No, because we're *idiots*, and clapping is what you do *after* someone has played a song on a real instrument!'

'But you've always said how good we are.'

'I was joking. I mean . . . we were, like . . . *six*. We've got to think about our reputations at school.'

'We don't *have* reputations.'

'Yeah, but I want one – and not as the freaky clapping guy.'

'C'mon, let's do "Rudolph", just for old time's sake. People didn't believe in Rudolph either, and then look what happened one foggy Christmas Eve.'

Jack gives me a withering look and stands. 'Sorry, Tom.' He pushes past and opens the garage door.

'Mum's making apple-and-rhubarb mini-muffins for after the show,' I say to his back.

He snaps his helmet on and rides off down the driveway.

'And warm cocoa,' I call out. 'I could ask if we can have marshmallows, too?'

I wait.

'See you tonight!' I shout into the street.

Jack does not look back.

I am side of stage, waiting. I'm surrounded by a bunch of Year One kids dressed as pumpkins, broccoli, zucchinis, carrots, kale and turnips. Their teacher, Mrs Mac, whispers loudly to them, 'Remember, root vegetables in the back row. And follow my cue for that tricky key change.'

'Would you please put your hands together,' says Mr Skroop, standing in the middle of the stage, 'for our next act . . . The Vegies!'

The little kids scurry onto the stage and I am left alone in the wings. I peek out, hoping to see Jack, hoping he's just trying to scare me by showing up at the last moment. Because he's doing a pretty good job. I can't see him, but I can see Sasha with her dad, sitting in the third row. Last time I performed for them I almost got chargrilled by a clown.

The CLAPPERS performing
their legendary 2016 gig

I can't do this. But I'm too scared to pull
out because of Skroop. The Christmas Concert
is his baby. (Before he became a teacher he
aspired to become a professional bagpipe
player.) Only a maniac would mess it up.

The Vegies perform 'We Wish You a Vegie
Christmas' and 'Jingle Bell Wok'. The audience
explodes. Mothers dry their eyes. It's a standing
ovation. No eggplant or brussels sprout has ever

been loved like this. I'm poked in the eye by the tip of a carrot as the kids rush offstage, buzzing.

'Ready to go?' the stage manager asks. He's a teenager with a beard of pimples. He clips the microphone to the neck of my tuxedo T-shirt. 'Run this cord down there and put the mic pack in your back pocket. Aren't there supposed to be two of you?'

'No,' I say, my stomach churning like a wave pool. 'Just one.'

'Weren't they just wonderful?' Mr Skroop says to the audience. 'Now, a last-minute inclusion. The much-loved Year Three riverdancers are, unfortunately, unable to perform this evening so, instead, we have . . .' He lowers his voice to a snarl. 'The Clappers.'

He struts offstage in the other direction. The crowd doesn't know whether to clap or not. Some of them do. The wave pool in my stomach grows into a tsunami.

'That's you!' the stage manager whispers, nudging me in the back, but my feet feel like they're bolted to the floor.

Skroop, in the other wing, motions angrily for me to get out there, but I can't move.

The school hall is silent.

'Go!' the pimply kid behind me whispers. I feel a hard shove from behind, and I fall out onto the stage on all fours. I look up at the crowd. There is scattered laughter. A teacher in the front row gets out of her seat to check that I'm okay. I stand. I gaze into the crowd, blinded by the stage lights. I can only see the first four rows clearly. Then an ocean of darkened heads.

If you ever have the chance to skip a day of school in exchange for performing solo in front of hundreds of people, I recommend you go to school.

'Go, Tom!' a kid calls from up the back. It sounds like Jonah Flem. A bunch of kids laugh.

'Whoo! I love you, Tom!' a girl screams. I'm pretty certain it's Stella Holling, the only girl who has ever loved me.

My brain tells me to start clapping but my body is way too smart for that.

Brain: Do it! They'll think you're an idiot if you just stand there.

Body: They'll think I'm a bigger idiot if I clap by myself and it's terrible.

Brain: Well, you need to do something. Do you know any jokes?

Body: Do you know any jokes?

Brain: Not off the top of my head.

Someone at the back starts a slow clap.

At first it's just a few kids, but pretty soon it's parents, grandparents and teachers. It gets faster and faster and faster. I turn to Mr Skroop in the wings, and he's clapping and grinning that evil grin like this is the best night of his life. He's finally got me.

I feel like I'm about to bawl my eyes out when the audience abruptly stops clapping. There is a single clap from behind me, on the stage. I figure it's Pimply Stage Guy, the genius who pushed me out here. I turn to scowl at him, but ...

It's Jack Danalis.

My ex-best friend.

And possibly 'best' again, depending on how this goes. Jack moves to the centre of the stage, clapping the opening bars of 'Jingle Bells' and, without thinking, I join in.

Jack thunders the baseline with big, cupped hands, and I patter over the top with a snappy, rapid-fire beat. Jack doubles his pace and I halve mine. Pretty soon I forget about the crowd. I forget about the day off tomorrow. I forget about Mum telling us we stink. I forget about Skroop in that dark cloak with the red eyes telling us we are 'insignificant, flat-footed, jelly-back-boned, knock-kneed little prawns'. I disappear inside The Clappers.

We finish with a punch – the most ferocious 30 seconds of Christmas carol clapping the world has ever seen. And then we're done.

I look out and notice the crowd for the first time in a couple of minutes. They stare at us – not in a good way.

Jack whispers, 'I'm going to kill you for this.'

They start booing. Raph Atkins, one of my friends, throws a hot dog at me. Then Luca Kingsley, the kid next to him, throws a half-eaten meat pie with sauce. Food rains down on the stage. The booing is so loud –

That's what I see and hear anyway.

What actually happens, after that stunned pause, is . . . they clap.

All of them.

The whole audience.

They stand and clap and scream and whistle twice as loudly as they cheered for The Vegies. The roar of it all echoes off the aluminium ceiling of the hall. Jack starts laughing like a madman – and so do I.

We take a bow and they cheer us as we

You too can have MAD clapping skills!
(A handy step-by-step GUIDE)

Step 1 Move hands together in a quick MANNER so they 'slap' each other.

Step 2 REPEAT (Don't wait too long!)

Step 3 LAUGH for Joy at your NEWLY learned SKILL

Ha
Ha
Ha
Ha

Step 4 Practice !!! (so you DON'T FORGET)

Step 5 Watch people GASP in amazement.

whoa!

Incredible.

That's dumb.

head offstage. We pass Skroop on our way to the wings. I swear I see flames leap from his deep, red eyes, but in real life this time.

'Quiet. Quiet please!' Skroop barks into the microphone. 'That's quite enough. Now, our final act for the evening –'

But the crowd won't quieten. The applause swells again, louder than before, drowning out Skroop's voice. 'Our final *act* –' he begins again, and someone in the crowd calls, 'More!' A bunch of others join in. From the side of the stage I can see Sasha and her dad and a bunch of kids from our class calling for more, so we head back out onstage. Skroop turns and waves us away, but the audience keeps shouting 'More!' until Skroop throws up his hands and returns to the wings.

'Um . . .' I say. 'We'll play you one of our favourites, "Rudolph the Red-Nosed Reindeer".'

The audience cheers again until Jack and I start up, and they fall silent. They watch. We haven't played it in a couple of years, so we're a bit rusty in the opening bars, but we give it everything we've got. We go like the clappers. I have to say, it feels pretty good up here. Dark room, bright lights, big crowd. I could get used to this. If I squint we could be playing Madison Square Garden or Wembley Stadium, and when the song is done, we swim offstage on a tidal wave of applause.

We sign kids' hands for them outside the hall after the show, and some audience members ask if we'll have photos taken with them. Most kids want a high-five, but Jack

THE Clappers

and I really need to be careful with our hands. Lots of people tell us we were the best act of the night, and Jack and I decide that this is the greatest day of our lives so far.

We meet up early the next morning at Jack's to shoot a Clappers video of us doing the Pink Panther theme song. It rocks. We upload it and then go to school, even though we don't have to. We figure we owe it to our fans.

Jack puts gel in his hair in case anyone wants a photo with him, and we each have a pen to sign autographs. (It's really annoying when someone wants an autograph and they don't have a pen.) We're both wearing gloves to protect our million-dollar palms.

But things seem kind of different today. By that I mean no one even mentions the concert. Except us.

We tell everyone about our video, but they're all watching a dumb video of Luca Kingsley's shaved, pink-skinned cat having a fight with a cactus instead. The cat is wearing mini red boxing gloves.

Jonah Flem says, 'You guys were great and all, but that boxing cat! Funniest thing I've ever seen.'

By the time I go to bed that night we have had 12 views. Most of them by us.

Not exactly viral. 'Cactus Cat' has had 732.
Life is unpredictable and sometimes cruel.

Still, we'll always have the Christmas
Concert. Almost every day of the school

holidays Jack says to me, 'Remember that night when we were stars and everyone loved us and we got to sign autographs?'

And that feels good. It really, really does.

Ten Reasons Why You Should Not Read the First Three Books About My Life:

1. They're full of dum stuff and will make you even stupider than you are now.

2. They feature angry teachers and parents, which is totally unrealistic because teachers and parents are never angry.

3. They tell more stories about Stella Holling, the girl who's always trying to kiss me – and kissing girls is weird and sick and wrong.

4. They document all my failed businesses, like my backyard theme park, my tooth mine and my pop-up school playground freak show.

5. They feature my weirdest body parts. (I don't know why I thought it was a good idea to write stories about my freaky four-toed foot, my big fat hairy birthmark and my appendix being ripped out of my body, but I did.)

6. Some stories will seriously mess with your mentals, like the day I woke up and everything was hovering.

7. Your teachers will probably take them off you and tell you to read something more intelligent, like *Just Stupid!* or *Captain Underpants and the Big, Bad Battle of the Bionic Booger Boy Part One: The Night of the Nasty Nostril Nuggets*.

8. Reading is good for you. Teachers and parents love it when you read, because it makes you smart, and then you'll get a good job and make lots of money and become famous and contribute to society. Which means that, when you read, parents and teachers are winning. Which means that you are losing, so you should not read in order to become more dum, and then you win. Ha!

9. *My Life & Other Stuff I Made Up* has a story about my nan and Jack's nan fighting in a back-alley brawl. It has the second-most disgusting end to a story in the history of

children's literature. (The grossest is the story about Brent Bunder's sore in *My Life & Other Stuff that Went Wrong*.)

10. You should be reading nourishing stuff, like Dickens and Shakespeare and Emily Brontë, not the ravings of a dum kid like me, who can't even spell 'dum'.

Peace.

I'm a really good reader...

nitrobobathylapherin?

RUNAWAY CAR

I hear the loud, non-stop honking of an old-fashioned car horn out front, and my heart sinks. It sounds like a flock of wounded geese. I should ignore it. I need to ignore it. But I don't. I go to the door and open it a crack. The heat of the day smacks me in the face and boils my eyeball juice. It's 40 degrees, the hottest day of summer so far. Nan is sitting in the driver's seat of a long, wide, shiny, light-blue 1952 Ford Crestline. A classic.

She honks the horn again and shouts, 'Come on, Tommy! Let's go for a drive.'

I open the door a little more and call out, 'It's too hot, Nan. I can't. Why don't you come inside and rest your weary bunions?'

She honks again. If Pop were alive he'd be furious that Nan was driving his pride and joy. Pop always kept the car garaged, shining it and tinkering with the engine, but he never drove it on the road. Now that he's gone, Nan likes to take it for a spin every now and then.

I wish Mum was home. She had to work today. There's no way she'd let me go with Nan. My grandmother is Australia's worst driver. Her top speed is 15 kilometres an hour. She drives so slowly that she makes time go backwards. She's a danger to herself and others. Last time I rode with her she mowed

Nan driving (this is <u>NOT</u> a driverless car).

down a stop sign, sideswiped a parked police car and smashed into the birdbath in the front yard of Mr Li's house at number 33.

She waves me over towards the car.
I shouldn't go, but I feel sorry for her – so skinny and frail in that gigantic vehicle. I take a deep breath, hurry down the front steps and along the path. She has the Crestline sitting half on the kerb, half on the street.

'Hello, Tommy, love. Give your ol' Nan a kiss.' I lean through the passenger window. She looks like a little kid at the wheel. She has to sit on three fat phone books from 1984 just to see over the dashboard. Nan climbs off the books and shuffles across the seat so I can kiss her on the cheek. Her skin is soft and wrinkled and sweaty. The car's engine rumbles and grumbles and burbles. Steam hisses from the cracks around the edge of the bonnet. Pop must be spinning in his grave.

'You really shouldn't be driving, Nan,' I tell her.

'Why not?'

'You don't have a licence.'

'When I was a girl, you didn't need a licence. I've been driving since I was seven years old.'

'I didn't know cars were invented then.'

'Don't be a smartypants,' she says. 'Back in my day, I could reverse a tractor through a flock of sheep blindfolded. Don't you trust me?'

No is the answer, but she gets really mad when I question her driving skills.

'Yes, Nan, I trust you. It's just that . . . I've got homework. I –'

'Rubbish. You've never done homework in your life. Now get in. I'll buy you an iceblock and take you to the swimming pool.'

Sweat runs in ticklish rivers down the sides of my face. The sun grills the skin on my forehead like cheese on toast. I think about her offer. I weigh up the fear and embarrassment of being in the car with her against the sweet relief of the pool and the iceblock.

I open the passenger door and slide in.

'That's my boy,' she says, grinning and revving the engine twice.

I reach for my seatbelt and try to find the socket to slot it into, but it's not there.

'Must have fallen down the crack between the seats, love. Not to worry. Off we go.'

She jerks forward and I'm thrown back against the seat. I plunge my arm down into the seat crack. I find an old Mintie with sand all over it and a 'One Penny' coin before I find the socket for the belt. I pull it up, slot it in and tighten it until my guts are about to squeeze out of my ears.

'You have nothing to worry about,' she says.

She stomps on the accelerator, the tyres squeal, and we shoot out from the kerb.

A car going by honks its horn and swerves, narrowly missing us.

Nan honks back. 'Nincompoop!' she screams. 'Sorry about that, Tommy. There are some crazy drivers on these roads.'

My Nan

81A38
CITY
POLICE

Worst driver
in Australia

I pull my belt tighter and the car settles into Nan's 15-kilometre-an-hour crawl up the hill.

'Nan, the pool's at the other end of the street.'

'I thought I'd get your iceblock from Papa Bear's. You can eat it on the way. How does that sound?'

'Thanks, Nan,' I say as we continue to climb. Papa Bear's is the shop up the hill on the corner of our street. My legs are sticking to the old vinyl seats in the heat, but it's quite nice going this speed. You notice stuff you wouldn't normally. Like that cat that just overtook us.

Oh no. My stomach sinks.

Brent Bunder and Jonah Flem are waiting to cross the street with their bikes about

40 metres up the hill. I slump down in my seat so I can't be seen.

'What're you doing?' Nan asks.

'It's comfy like this,' I tell her. 'Cooler.' I look up and notice that the clouds are moving faster than we are.

'Can you go any slower, Grandma?' Jonah calls out as we drive by.

'Shut your gob, pipsqueak!' Nan screams. 'Respect your elders.'

Brent and Jonah laugh.

'Hey, is that you, Weekly?' Brent asks.

I slide down further into the seat.

'Hey, Weekly!' he calls.

The two boys pedal slowly alongside the car, looking down at me.

'Nice Sunday drive, mate?' Jonah asks. 'Why don't you just walk? It'd be faster.'

Nan swerves to the right and bumps one of their bikes. I sit up and look back to see Jonah checking his front wheel. 'Hey!' he shouts. 'You're a danger to society, lady!'

'Your face is a danger to mirrors!' Nan shouts back, peering through the steering wheel as we crawl up the hill. 'That showed them.'

Just me and Nan on a leisurely Sunday drive.

'Nan, you're not really supposed to knock kids' bikes.'

'They're not kids. They're cane toads. There's no law against squishing a couple of cane toads, is there?'

I shrug. Flem and Bunder are kind of cane toad-ish. But the police might not see it that way if they report her. A few minutes later we roll up outside Papa Bear's. Nan slams into the rear bumper of the car parked out front, then rolls back downhill a few centimetres.

'There we go,' she says. 'What do you want, love? A Bubble O' Bill?'

Nan knows that I love Bubble O' Bills more than life itself. Especially on a flesh-meltingly hot day like today. I nod and grin.

'Two Bubble O' Bills coming right up.' She grabs her purse, climbs down off the phone books, exits the car and slams the door. She slams it so hard that the car wobbles from side to side. There's a screeking sound of metal on metal, the suspension groans, and the car starts to roll slowly backwards.

'Nan!' I shout, but she's shuffling along in front of the car now and doesn't hear me.

I look to the dashboard and see a handle that says 'Park Brake' in faded white lettering. I reach across and yank it hard. The handle heaves back towards me . . . and snaps off in my hand. I scream and throw the handle into the back seat.

'Nan!'

She disappears inside the shop and I'm picking up speed. I've rolled about five metres down the hill and I'm heading towards a silver hatchback parked on the kerb. I could open

the door and jump out, but I'd hit the gutter
pretty hard.

I peel my sweaty legs off the seat and
slide across until my hip hits the pile of
phone books. I jerk the wheel to the right in
a desperate attempt to miss the parked car.
The back of Nan's car veers out into the road
and another car swerves around me,
the driver slamming his fist on the horn.
I'm heading diagonally across the street now,
so I pull the wheel back towards me to stay
on the left side of the road.

I'm really moving now. I chuck the phone
books onto the passenger floor and slide
behind the wheel. I'm looking back over my
shoulder and trying to steer, but I haven't
driven a car recently – or ever – so it's a bit
difficult. My feet are tap dancing, trying to

find the brake pedal. It must be down there somewhere.

Jonah and Brent are in the middle of the road.

'Get out of the way!' I shout out the window. I look for the horn and slam my fist down on the big 'Ford' logo in the middle of the steering wheel.

Waaaaaaaarp! The horn blurts.

I look back through the rear windscreen. Brent and Jonah look up at the car speeding towards them. We all scream.

I AM ALONE IN MY GRANDMOTHER'S CAR, TEARING BACKWARDS DOWN KINGSLEY STREET TOWARDS THE TWO TOUGHEST KIDS IN MY CLASS.

IS THERE ANY WAY I'LL MAKE IT OUT ALIVE?

FIND OUT IN:

Eating is my favourite extreme sport.

MY LIFE AND OTHER WEAPONISED MUFFINS

TOM WEEKLY

MY LIFE AND OTHER WEAPONISED MUFFINS

AS TOLD TO TRISTAN BANCKS AND GUS GORDON

My mum's raspberry muffins are weapons of **minor destruction**. I've been **trapped inside a runaway car** on a trip to buy ice cream. I accidentally invented **meatball bungee**. And my recipe for chocolate mousse has a **secret ingredient** that you don't even want to know.

What Would You Rather Do?

1. Ride a shark or a rhino?
2. Kiss a dog or a cat?
3. Get a needle in the eye or have your bum set on fire?

hee hee

hee

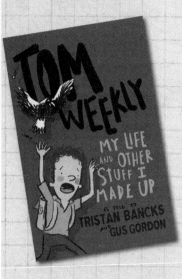

This is a nail-biting
— make that toe-biting —
thrill ride through my life.

MY LIFE AND OTHER STUFF I MADE UP

This is where I pour out
whatever's inside my head.
Like the time a **bloodthirsty magpie** was
out to get me. Or when I had to **eat Vegemite
off my sister's big toe.** And don't forget the day
I ate **67 hot dogs** in ten minutes. My life gets a bit
weird sometimes, but that's how I roll.

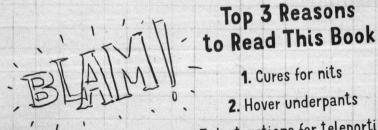

Top 3 Reasons to Read This Book

1. Cures for nits

2. Hover underpants

3. Instructions for teleporting

If you want to know what went wrong, read this and laugh.

MY LIFE AND OTHER STUFF THAT WENT WRONG

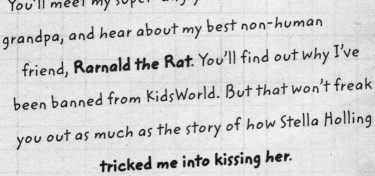

You'll learn the secret of my **strangest body part.** You'll meet my super-angry grandpa, and hear about my best non-human friend, **Rarnald the Rat.** You'll find out why I've been banned from KidsWorld. But that won't freak you out as much as the story of how Stella Holling **tricked me into kissing her.**

Things You'll Learn

1. How to climb Mount Everest

2. How to make a backyard theme park

3. How to escape a pirate

this plACE JOLLY well stinks !!

You think you've made mistakes?
I've made more.

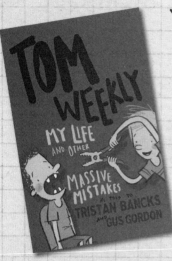

MY LIFE AND OTHER MASSIVE MISTAKES

Every single word in this book is true. I do know someone with the **worst case of nits** in history. Stella Holling used chocolate to trick me into kissing her **again**. My sister, Tanya, truly is an evil genius. And as weird as it sounds, I really did ask Jack to help me **mine my teeth** for cash. It's embarrassing, **but it's true**.

YOU DID

WHAT??!

Bonus Stuff Inside

1. Make your own slime

2. Meet the world's freakiest cat

3. Test for Cranky Dad Syndrome

Acknowledgements

There are many people who contribute in big and small ways to the making of a book. Thanks to my first readers, Huxley and Luca Bancks and Claire and Raph Atkins for your insights, encouragement and humour. Thanks to Paul McMahon for brainstorming fat cats with me. And Amber Melody for inspiring me.

I love interacting and collaborating with the readers of my books. I often throw a new story idea out to students when I visit a school and we brainstorm ideas together. Thanks to all the teachers, librarians, booksellers and readers who support me but especially to Mountain Creek SHS years 7 & 8 students, St Andrews Lutheran College, Noosa District State High School, Flinders CCC years 4, 5 and 6, Grand Avenue SS year 4, St Dominic's PS,

Huntingtower School year 4, Moomba Park PS, Beaconhills College Berwick, Genesis Christian College, Frank Partridge VC PS, Nambucca Valley Community Christian School, Caulfield Grammar Junior School, MacGregor SS, Aitken College year 6, Springfield Anglican College, St Bernardine's PS, Brisbane Boys' College year 5, Shailer Park SHS year 7, St Josephs Terrace year 7, Sandy Beach PS, Newington College Lindfield and St Gabriels PS year 6.

Thanks for special input online and in sessions from Abbey, Ansh, Isobelle, Chloe, Amelia, Aidan, Ryan, Hayden, Tynan, William, Mitchell, Dr Carpet, Robert, Tara, Jacob, Faith, Harmony, Isaac, Rob, Layla, Amy, Elijah, Fjord, Kaleb, Jed, Tyler, Trinity, Abby, Ely, Rachel, Olivia, Lauren, Mehret, Joel, Hunter, Charlotte, Tim, Hayden, Maddie, Elly, Adrian, Ryan, Amelia, Kayla, Kai, Laura, Lilya, Ruby, Xavier, Isaac, Jonah, Ray, Alana, Katie, Tony,

Dominique, Shaniah, Ruby, Hugo, Finn, Banjo, Maja, Nicholas, Miriam, Reuben, Tansy, Grace, Sophie, Christopher, Felix, Daniel, Meg, Sophia, Max and Jayde.

Thanks to LitVids book trailer participants and the 2015 Splendour in the Grass brainstormers. And to Cathy Shay, Tamara Rodgers, Natalie LaRocque, M Fenely, Deborah Hogg and Demelza Dean for insights into librarian life.

And a huge thank you to Anthony Blair and Jo Butler at Cameron's and the amazing team at Penguin Random House Australia who help make the *My Life* series as weird, funny and gross as it can be and who help put my books into readers' hands: Zoe Walton, Brandon VanOver, Julie Burland, Dot Tonkin, Zoe Bechara, Angela Duke and Mary van Reyk.

About the Author

Tristan Bancks is a children's and teen author with a background in acting and filmmaking. His books include the Tom Weekly series, Mac Slater series and crime-mystery novels for middle-graders, including *Two Wolves* (*On the Run* in the US) and *The Fall*. *Two Wolves* won Honour Book in the 2015 Children's Book Council of Australia Book of the Year Awards and was shortlisted for the Prime Minister's Literary Awards. It also won the YABBA and KOALA Children's Choice Awards. Tristan is a writer-ambassador for the literacy charity Room to Read. He is excited by the future of storytelling and inspiring others to create. Visit Tristan at tristanbancks.com

About the Illustrator

Gus Gordon has written and illustrated over 70 books for children. He writes books about motorbike-riding stunt chickens, dogs that live in trees, and singing on rooftops in New York. His picture book *Herman and Rosie* was a 2013 CBCA Honour Book. Gus loves speaking to kids about illustration, character design and the desire to control a wiggly line. Visit Gus at gusgordon.com

Room to Read®

About Room to Read

Tristan Bancks is a committed writer-ambassador for Room to Read, an innovative global non-profit that has impacted the lives of over ten million children in ten low-income countries through its Literacy and Girls' Education programs. Room to Read is changing children's lives in Bangladesh, Cambodia, India, Laos, Nepal, South Africa, Sri Lanka, Tanzania, Vietnam and Zambia – and you can help!

In 2012 Tristan started the Room to Read World Change Challenge in collaboration with Australian school children to build a school library in Siem Reap, Cambodia. Over the years since Tristan, his fellow writer-ambassadors and kids in both Australia and Hong Kong have raised $80,000 to buy 80,000 books for children in low-income countries.

For more information or to join this year's World Change Challenge, visit tristanbancks.com/p/change-world.html, and to find out more about Room to Read, visit roomtoread.org.